Two Animal Rights Stories

Two Animal Rights Stories

Tell Me Your Story
&
The Risks of Empathy

Rick Bogle

Virginia Smith
BOOKS

Tell Me Your Story was originally published in 2009.
The Risks of Empathy was originally published in 2012.
Both have been slightly revised.

ISBN-13: 978-0692916087
ISBN-10: 0692916083

Rick Bogle

Tell Me Your Story

In his thoughts, Herman spoke a eulogy for the mouse who had shared a portion of her life with him and who, because of him, had left this earth. "What do they know—all these scholars, all these philosophers, all the leaders of the world—about such as you? They have convinced themselves that man, the worse transgressor of all species, is the crown of creation. All other creatures were created merely to provide him with food, pelts, to be tormented, exterminated. In relation to them, all people are Nazis; for the animals it is an eternal Treblinka."

Issac Bashevis Singer (1902–1991)
"The Letter Writer"
From *The Séance and Other Stories*, 1968

The First Part

The trees were budding out; a few early pink blossoms punctuated the iridescence of the gold and purple new leaves. The sun glowed warmly and had coaxed a few early dandelions to add their beauty to the already lush hillside meadow. Rudy was lying with his head on his rolled-up and now unneeded sweater. The remnants of their simple picnic lunch were still strewn about the blanket. Other picnicking couples were also lying around soaking up the early spring warmth. He watched Cindy and a few of her girl friends tossing a Frisbee and gamboling about. It was idyllic.

His fiancé threw the red disk, shouted something to her friends, turned, and smiling, ran up the low hill to their blanket. As she ran, Rudy couldn't help but recall his father's one criticism of his only son's choice in a future wife. "She has no bosom," he had complained. "Children need a large bosom to provide them the rich milk they need to grow up big and strong." But Rudy would have nothing of it. Though Cindy was slight, and far from the ideal mother-figure held up by society, her high cheek bones, perfect teeth, her beautiful golden hair, and piercing blue eyes were, even Rudy's father had to admit, the image of a true Aryan angel.

Breathing heavily from her exertions, Cindy collapsed onto the blanket and threw her arm around Rudy. "What an incredibly beautiful day!" she said. "I don't want it to end." She rolled over onto her back, closed her eyes, and relaxed with a deep and contented sigh. "Is there any wine left?"

"Maybe a glass. We'll share it."

Cindy heard Rudy rummaging in the basket, the clink of a glass, and the pop of the cork.

"Here sweetheart."

She opened one eye and took the glass of white wine. She raised her head to take a sip. "What's this?" she said, and cast a glance at Rudy who was feigning confusion and surprise. Something gold was shimmering at the bottom. She dipped her finger into the glass and pulled out a finely fashioned chain that had a gold swastika dangling from it. At the center was a tiny diamond; on the back was an inscription: To my sweetest Cindy. 75th World Reich Day. Rudy

"Rudolph Hess Schwartz, it's beautiful. I love you so much! I can't wait until we're married."

Dr. Archibald Nelson had decided to spare no expense on his daughter's wedding. Because she was marrying into the main Aryan line, he knew that he would be expected to invite every party dignitary the Schwartz's knew, and that was many. In addition, he knew that his entire family would be under close observation during the party – the not so subtle inquiries into his family's history and racial background had begun the moment Rudy and Cindy had announced their engagement. But Archie wasn't worried. The Nelsons, though not of German or Austrian descent, could trace their heritage back to South Carolina and a particularly large plantation and large slave holding, a feature that the World Reich Bürokratie looked on as a sign of good moral character since it upheld the purity of the races.

Archie was still surprised at the doors that had begun to open for him. He had already received an offer to join the staff at the prestigious Joseph Mengele Memorial Hospital for Genetic and Racial Disease of Chicago, an offer he knew he could hardly turn down. And Cindy had already been admitted to the Reich University of Illinois, an institution well above the aspirations of anyone not of Master Race descent or otherwise intimately affiliated with the Reich.

No expense would be spared. He would make sure that when Cindy stood at the alter with Rudy, that every head would nod in approval, that even though she might not be certifiably a member of the Master Race, there could be no doubt that her family was of the very best New World Caucasian stock and that their children would be highly valuable additions to the World Reich.

Tell Me Your Story

In late 1942, the battle for Stalingrad was not going well for the Nazis. The Russians had rallied and had cornered nearly 300,000 German and Romanian soldiers in a pincer movement that left them bottled up in the city. At the same time, the aerial Blitzkrieg aimed at Britain had stalled. America was proving to be a more formidable foe than the German generals had imagined, and some secretly advised that the multiple fronts were proving more difficult than had been predicted and having to fight on many fronts might even lead to the unthinkable possibility of defeat.

The now well-known story is that Hitler had for some time been hoping to win the war on the ground. No one questioned whether one-on-one a German soldier was the fiercest and best warrior on the planet, but the odds were becoming increasingly difficult. Hitler's hopes of a conventional victory that would have bestowed infinite honor on the German army had finally been dashed by the realities of the Russian resistance and counter offensive. And, as every school child now learns, it was with a heavy heart, but with infinite love for the Master Race, that he ordered the commencement of the top-secret vulkanische Eruption des Betriebes, or Operation Volcanic Eruption.

On January 1, 1943, the first Atombombe was dropped on Moscow, and the eastern front was won. In spite of photographs and descriptions of the magnitude of the destruction and of Germany's new awesome power being sent to London and Washington along with demands of immediate surrender, the British and the Americans intensified their air attacks on German positions in Western Europe. On February 1, 1943, the second Atombombe was dropped on London. In spite of photographs and another demand for immediate surrender, the Americans, apparently thinking their country was protected by the Atlantic, defied Hitler's demands and fought on. On March 1, flying from a secret air base in Greenland, a German bomber dropped the third Atombombe on New York and the fourth on Washington DC. The war was effectively over. Hitler then declared war on Italy, which surrendered immediately, and on Japan, which resisted until the fifth and final Atombombe was dropped on Hiroshima on April 1. On May 1, 1943, Adolph Hitler formally declared the establishment of the World Reich and demanded that deputations from every country, now referred to as World Reich Zuständes, attend the first World Reich Congress in Berlin. And, thus, the 1000-Year World Reich was officially convened.

Rudolph Hess Schwartz could trace his family tree back into the dim early history of the Rhineland. His paternal great grandfather, Heinz Wilhelm Schwartz, had been a hero in the war who had led a Panzer tank division that routed a French army battalion and rescued a captured German army company. His maternal great grandfather, Günther Schaafhausen had been an assistant to the legendary Rudolph Hess. His parents met during their early years as minor officials in the World Reich Korps der globalen Verwalter, the bureaucratic corps that oversaw politics in the Zuständes. Their successes had led to each of them being assigned to the central North American Reich Command in Chicago, considered a strudel of an assignment, early in their careers. They fell in love and had four children. Rudy was the youngest, the only male, and last to marry.

Archie arrived for his interview at the Joseph Mengele Memorial Hospital for Genetic and Racial Disease promptly at 9:00AM. He was greeted by Dr. Otto Eckel, Chief of Staff who clicked his heals sharply in greeting.

"Dr. Nelson! Heil Hitler! It is a pleasure to meet you finally."

"The Reich! The Führer! It is a great honor sir!"

"This interview is just a formality, of course," said Dr. Eckel. "Mainly, I just wanted to show you around, introduce you to the staff and those you will be working with, and welcome you to Joseph Mengele."

"I have always dreamed of being able to work here, Herr Eckel."

"Excellent. Come with me."

The Nelsons were preparing to eat their Sunday dinner. Archie was carving a ham. Trish brought out the last dish, an old ceramic blue Delph bowl of steaming green beans and set it on the table amid the mashed potatoes, bread, and salad. Already seated were Mary, Cindy's ten-year-old sister, Cindy, and Rudy, who had become a regular fixture at the Nelsons' Sunday table.

"Oh Daddy, you should see the pictures of the resort we're staying at in Bavaria. Schloss Neuschwanstein. It's a real castle. It's the most exclusive hotel in the Alps; only the best people get to stay there. It's like something out of a fairy tale. Rudy's mom and dad stayed there on their honeymoon too," said Cindy. "It's beautiful! Mom says she's jealous; maybe you guys can go there sometime too."

"Wait till we say grace Mary," warned Trish Nelson when her young daughter reached for a slice of the warm crusty bread. "And everyone leave a little room for apple pie. We have ice cream too."

"I always have room for your pie Mrs. Nelson," said Rudy; he squeezed Cindy's hand under the table.

Archie sat down. "Cindy, why don't you say grace."

Everyone bowed their head. "Dear Lord, thank you for the food we are about to eat and for all the wonderful things you have given us. Thank you for my wonderful fiancé. Thank you for Daddy's new job. Thank you for our wonderful World Reich. Thank you for everything Lord. Heil Hitler. Amen."

"Heil Hitler. Amen," repeated the family.

"Now, Mary," said her mother, "Take a slice of bread and pass the plate to Rudy."

"We're flying to Munich right after the wedding and taking a train to Hohenschwangau. Rudy's cousin Hans is going to pick us up at the station and take us to the hotel."

"It sounds so exciting," said Trish. "Doesn't it dear?"

Archie looked down the table at everyone's plate. "Pass your plate down Rudy, and I'll give you another slice of ham. Honey, the raisin sauce is the best you've made. Did you change recipes?"

"Mom, can I go over to Judy's after dinner?" Mary asked her mother.

"You were there last night, Mary." she answered, "Why not have her over here instead?"

"Ok."

That night, the Nelson's were lying in bed together. They had just turned out the light and Trish said, "You were in a mood tonight."

"What do you mean?"

"Well, twice, you changed the subject. You didn't answer me when I said the honeymoon sounded exciting, and then later, when Cindy asked about your new job, you changed the subject again. Why?"

"I'm just stressed. Right now the best thing will be to see that the wedding goes well and Cindy and Rudy get settled in when they get back."

"Is that really it? It seems like something else is bothering you. Is it something about Rudy? Or your job?"

"You know how much I like Rudy. Cindy couldn't have found a better husband. He's smart, kind, comes from a good German family and really loves Cindy."

"And the new job?"

"It's getting late. Let's go to sleep."

Rebbe Shrinkle was standing in the darkest corner of a darkcellar. A tiny candle cast a tiny glow that was shielded as well as possible by the seven people standing with him. He finished his hushed recitation of the Havdalah and passed the small cup of wine.

"Thank you Rebbe."

Rebbe Shrinkle slipped out of his vestments. He rolled the prayer book into his robe, took back the small cup, each of the men's yamakas, and put everything into his large fur hat. Two men helped him lift a part of the concrete slab. He put everything into the hidden niche and helped them lower the heavy piece of concrete back into place. A woman opened a small plastic bag with the dust and grime that had been swept from the slab only an hour ago. She cast the contents on the floor and everyone spread the dust around with their feet. She sprinkled around some cracked corn. The rats would come after the secret worshipers had left and obliterate their footprints.

Rebbe Shrinkle blew out the small candle and set it on its side on a narrow ledge at the top of the wall. They stood together in the dark.

"Rebbe, my daughter says she doesn't believe that her friends will stop liking her if they learn she is a Jew. I keep telling her to shut up. I've tried to reason with her. I don't know what to do."

"She must not tell," said the Rebbe. "You must tell her more of our story; give her more examples of our struggle to survive. You must paint a more realistic picture for her. You must get on your knees and beg if you have to."

"Now. Everyone. We must go now. I will see you again in 20 days. Shalom. God be with you."

Rebbe Shrinkle stayed deep in the shadows until he was blocks away from the old warehouse. It wasn't likely that anyone else would be in this part of the city. Hitler had decreed that the cities destroyed by the Atombombes would remain as testaments to the Reich's power and a permanent reminder of its willingness to use it.

As a result, at each of the bombsites a deep crater remained, barren and unfilled. Concentric rings of lessoning destruction radiated outwards from ground zero until the destruction was more or less unnoticeable.

The Rebbe finally stepped into streetlights and merged unnoticed into the moderate crowd of pedestrians.

The wedding was held in the First German Lutheran Church of Chicago; the largest most prestigious church in the entire American Reich Zustände. Rudy's grandparents, many aunts, uncles, and cousins had flown in from Europe. Cindy's family had deep roots in the Chicago area; her large extended family was well represented. The senior medical and research staff from Joseph Mengele and many of Rudy's parents' colleagues from the World Reich bureaucratic corps were there too. Cindy and Rudy had invited many of their own friends. Nearly 400 people watched as Cindy walked up the long aisle with her father and applauded as the couple drank from the traditional Nuernberg Wedding Cup.

Another hundred friends showed up for the formal reception. Archie looked around the room satisfied that the caterers and the hotel had done a masterful job. The band was playing just the right mix of traditional German and more modern selections. As he had hoped and planned, the many Reich dignitaries and guests did indeed nod their heads in clear approval at the richness of the event and the beauty of the bride in spite of her family not being of the Master Race.

Archie looked around the room again and reflected on the great financial cost. Though it would take many years for them to pay off the giant debt, he reckoned that the golden road to security that now lay ahead of his daughter and future grand children was more than worth the price. He accidentally let his thoughts drift to his new job, something he had promised himself he would not do on this special day, and a dark cloud descended over the ballroom. He was relieved when his wife came up from behind and dispelled his morose musings.

"Dance with me," she said.

Cindy had read about the Fatherland and had studied its illustrious history in school, but she was unprepared for the lavishness of German life. Germany and Austria lived on the toils of the rest of the planet. The Fatherland indulged in a luxury borne of power that could not have been imagined prior to the establishment of the World Reich.

Exports from the region were limited to uniquely German and Austrian products made by artisans and hobbyists. Other than a required two years in the globales Polizeikorps, the Master Race did not have to work; everything was freely available to them in the Fatherland. It was purely a sense of duty or adventure that motivated some, like Rudy's parents, to join the diplomatic corps and assume the leadership and control of the global government and economy or to look for other ways to serve the Reich around the world. Most Germans and Austrians were content to stay home, indulge in the arts, pursue philosophic ideals, and bask in the absolute unquestioned truth of their own immense superiority.

At the hotel and in the surrounding local restaurants and clubs, the newlyweds luxuriated in a servant-filled world of rich foods and entertainment beyond belief. Cindy tried to make a mental note of the many extraordinary extravagances to share with her mother and father, but in only a short time she realized that unless they experienced it themselves, there would be no way to really explain what being a member of the Master Race truly implied.

When Archie was offered the job at Joseph Mengele he had realized that it was an offer that he was not at liberty to refuse. At the same time, he did not want to lose his own family practice altogether so had negotiated one day a week that he could continue to see some of his patients. Though he had to help many of his long-time patients find a new physician, he was able to continue providing medical care for a few. Looking back, he thought that this connection with humanity might be the only thing keeping him sane.

The shock of his initial tour with Mengele Chief of Staff Otto Eckel, PhD., M.D., had seared a permanent wound into his soul; it was an experience he would not forget.

In the elevator, Dr. Eckel had begun discussing his new duties.

"Of course, you know, only German and Austrian doctors are licensed to treat the Race, but we have many non-Aryans who come to us for help, and when the case is particularly interesting, we are only too happy to try and help. Also, many of our staff, the nurses, the orderlies, the custodians, the kitchen staff, for instance, all get their basic health care from Mengele, so you will, from time to time, be asked to evaluate and treat them. Is that agreeable to you?"

"Of course, Herr Eckel. I had no illusions."

"Good. Your main job will be overseeing the medical care of our research colonies. We haven't been very happy with the doctors we've hired who have specialized in the field, and we are hoping that by assigning a physician with real clinical experience, that we will get a better result."

"I don't understand, Herr Doctor. I have no veterinary experience and wouldn't know how to treat a mouse or a rat."

"No, no. That's understandable. We don't use many lower animals here at Mengele any longer or at any other World Reich Research Center for that matter; they have proved quite unsuitable for our research; the results from the lower animals, even from monkeys and chimpanzees, have been completely misleading. When I stop to think of the years of wasted time and money and the diseases left misunderstood, the patients left to suffer, I am deeply thankful that clear-thinking German science has generally dispensed with such archaic means. Almost all of our research today is conducted on subhumans."

And, as if on cue, the elevator door opened onto what seemed more a prison hallway than any hospital Archie had ever visited.

Eckel was watching Archie closely. "Yes. The odor is disagreeable, but one can become accustomed to it. Sometimes I don't notice it at all."

He led the way out of the elevator and proceeded down the hallway. On each side were cells separated by solid concrete walls. The front of each cell was fashioned of iron bars. A metal bar with a handle protruded from the front wall at the edge of each cell. Down the hall, a man was pushing a cart and tossing a scoop of something into each cell.

"Ah, feeding time," said Eckel.

In each cell was a person. There didn't seem to be any pattern. Single men, single women, single boys and girls, one to each cell, naked and tough looking. Some were bald and had stitches in their heads; most had long hair snarled into dreadlocks. Some were bandaged; some had some sort of experimental device protruding from their body or head.

As the food was thrown into their cell, most gathered it up quickly and shoved it into their mouths. Some seemed unaware that anything had been thrown into their cell, some were screaming, others moaning, some sat huddled while a few were pacing rapidly back and forth picking up a piece of kibble at each pass.

Eckel couldn't help noticing the pallor that had come over Archie who stood as if frozen. "Yes, the colonies can be shocking the first time one sees them," said Eckel. "But the benefits to society far outweigh the costs, I'm sure you'll agree. We have Jews, Blacks, Asiatics, and a sprinkling of other subhuman races; it is really interesting work. We have discovered that each race is a uniquely productive model of certain illnesses or maladies afflicting the Master Race. Over the past fifty years we have seen amazing advances in medical science, as I'm sure you'll agree, eh Herr Doctor?"

Eckel had seen enough initial reactions to the colonies to recognize the need to get Dr. Nelson into a more comfortable setting. Back in his luxurious office, he offered him a shot of Schnapps.

"You won't be expected to spend much time on the actual colony floors, just look over charts and write orders for the workers. You might occasionally be asked to offer medical advice for a particular project and to treat the occasional serious case. I'm sure with time, you will come to feel proud at making an important contribution to medical knowledge."

Levi Sach sat on the thin foam pad in a back corner of his bleak steel and concrete cell. A pile of feces was in the other back corner. There was a red plastic ball against the wall. He could see the woman in the cell across from him, but she had not spoken to him or anyone else since she was brought in many days earlier.

She would look over when he spoke, so he knew she could hear him. Levi had once been across from a man for a long time who couldn't hear anything at all; he had learned to converse after a fashion with hand gestures. The deaf man sometimes twisted in an odd way, turning his head far to one side and rolling his eyes. His left arm would shake and twitch at the same time. The Germans came to his cell twice a day and made him swallow something. He always fought them.

The Germans came to Levi's cell only two or three times a week. They came to take a syringe of blood. He had learned over the years that cooperating with them was less painful, usually, than resisting. You couldn't stop them from doing anything to you, so fighting them was futile. He had seen many people try, but the Germans would just pull the lever on the side of the cell and the back wall of bars would slide forward, impossible to resist, and pin you against the front bars. Then they would inject you and you would go limp. There was no escape. No escape.

Trish took the roast out of the oven. Since her daughter's marriage to Rudy, she had been able to shop at special stores and to buy the best products at incredibly low prices. At her regular stores she was escorted into back rooms crowded with an assortment of goods that were never available to the regular shopper.

Tell Me Your Story

She set the table for Sunday dinner. Her youngest daughter was at a friend's house and due home at any time. She glanced at the old clock over the hutch and hurried back into the kitchen. As she stirred the gravy she wondered again about her husband. He hadn't been willing to talk about his new job. She could tell that he didn't like it; she could tell from his tossing and turning at night; she could tell from his few real smiles and his hollow laughter. She thought that he was probably mad and disappointed in the Nazi doctors at Joseph Mengele. They probably weren't giving him the respect he thought he deserved.

At night they could talk to each other. There were thirty cells in Levi's room. They were all being used. He had been brought to Joseph Mengele when he was six years old, but he didn't know how old he was. He knew nine of the people in the room quite well. They too had been in that room for a long time. The others were replaced frequently. Like him, the nine had blood taken every few days.

They spoke to each other in a hodge-podge of words, grunts, and organic syntax. The nine had language that was somewhat similar to the Germans'. Many of the room's residents had been born in the labs. Some had spent time when very young in isolation and manipulated environments. Some of them could barely communicate; most could make themselves understood, to a degree. Four of them wore vests – impossible to remove – that were attached to tethers and tubes emerging from the ceiling. These four did little but moan. But even among the rest there was a lot of moaning at night and throughout the day; lots of moaning, coughing, and sometimes screams.

"Are you going to get a new car Daddy? I know Mom wants one." Cindy and Rudy had resumed their Sunday dinners with her parents when they got back from their honeymoon. They had an apartment and were both at RUC, the Reich University of Chicago; "The Fighting SS."

"Mary, what's wrong?" asked Trish looking at her younger daughter.

"Sarah Johnson's mom told her she shouldn't play with me anymore."

"Why on earth would she say that?" asked Cindy.

"Her mother said that we're Master Race now and she's ordinary. Ordinary people and Master Race people don't like each other she said."

"Oh Mary, that's silly. I wasn't Master Race, and I married Rudy," Cindy said, casting a glance at her new husband. "It was hard sometimes, but ordinary people and the Master Race can get along with each other."

"Just tell her that you aren't really Master Race," said Rudy. "Your nieces and nephews will be," he gleamed at Cindy, "but you can't be, you never will be, you don't have German or Austrian blood. If she won't play with you, just let me know."

"Would someone please pass me the green beans?" interrupted Archie.

Cindy had been enjoying her first year at RUC. The lecture halls were very comfortable and her classmates wore all the latest fashions. There had been some friction at first when she revealed that she was from old Chicago stock and did not have the more common German and Austrian backgrounds of most of the students at RUC, but except for one or two haughty girls, everyone else seemed to quickly forget about her non-Aryan heritage.

One day, she went into her Modern Politics class and found a pamphlet on her chair; they were on all the chairs. She read through it as she waited for her professor to arrive.

On the front was a picture of a man strapped into chair of some sort with wires attached to something that seemed to be screwed into his head. There was a grimace on his face. The title of the brochure was Cruelty at RUC. The pamphlet claimed that there were secret labs on campus with Jews, blacks, and other "subhumans" being used in cruel experiments. It gave examples of what it called cruel experimentation. It said that students had a responsibility to ask questions and to speak out.

The class had entered into a loud and boisterous discussion about the pamphlet by the time Professor Kretschmer arrived. He was pelted with questions almost immediately.

"Herr Professor Kretschmer, have you seen this? What do you think about it? Is it true? So what? It's cruel. They're subhumans. We eat pigs and cows, what's the big deal? Isn't this just emotionalism? These people are anti-science!"

"Class! Class! Everyone settle down." The professor picked up the brochure that was lying on the lectern and looked it over quickly. "Every year or so someone or some small group of malcontents writes up something like this and distributes it around campus. As you can see, this is anonymous, so we can't ask the authors how they came to have these ideas.

"I've looked into these claims and have found them all to be completely misinformed and wildly confused. It is true that our scientists and researchers use a few subhumans in their research, but very strict rules govern everything about them. Subhumans are used only when it is absolutely necessary, only when there are no alternatives, and they always receive the very best care. They are treated like the best Germans in the best hospitals. There is a committee on campus that oversees all research using subhumans and makes sure that the research is very important and that all the regulations are followed. This trash makes it look like the scientists are monsters, and I can assure you that they are the most compassionate people in the world and are working hard to rid the world of disease.

"Now, let's move on to the last assigned reading." He looked down at his class roster, "Heinz Walkerling, please explain the authority structure of the North American Zustände."

Their new apartment was small but luxurious. Rudy's parents knew the building's owner. They were on the 63rd floor of Hermann Göring Tower, their small living room window and their bedroom window both looked out on Lake Michigan. They had just finished making love and were lying snuggled together under a black silk sheet.

"How was school today?" Rudy asked in almost a whisper. His face was against Cindy's head, buried in her hair.

Cindy's eyes were closed. She could feel Rudy's warm breath on her scalp. He felt her tense up slightly. "It was ok."

"Did something happen?" He was always a little worried that she might be subjected to some small uncomfortable discrimination.

"Not really. There was a sort of commotion in Politics. Someone had left a brochure about experiments on subhumans in all the seats. Professor Kretschmer said it was all wrong and that there are strict regulations. But the photos look real. I have it in my notebook."

She jumped out of bed and hurried to and from the living room. She got into bed, propped up her pillows, and pulled the sheet up around her. "Here it is."

Rudy sat up too and looked at the brochure. He read it through. "The pictures look real. Do you think they really do this stuff on campus?"

"I don't know. Kretschmer went on and on. He seemed a little mad. He said there are only a few subhumans on campus. Isn't it funny the way they put subhuman in quotation marks every time?"

"I wonder if we can find out what's actually going on? I'll ask around; don't you say anything about this. OK? It isn't good for you to stand out too much, and everyone already looks at you all the time because you are so god-damned beautiful."

He dropped the pamphlet off the bed and began kissing her again.

Drs. Ulrich Hamm and Frizt Kals were colleagues. Hamm was the head of the psychiatry department at Joseph Mengele Memorial Hospital for Genetic and Racial Disease and Kals was a senior scientist and professor at Reich University of Chicago. Together they had identified a distinct phenotype of Jew with trait-like extreme anxiety. They scientifically bred Jews with the trait and had recently characterized the gene, which they dubbed, f-HEB, or the fretting-Homolog of Fearful Behavior. Informally, they called it the "Hebe gene."

Dr. Kals ran a large MRI center on campus. Together the scientists had developed a protocol that was letting them look piece by piece at living brains. They would first train a Jew with the f-HEB genotype to choose one of three food items. The subject was restrained in a chair-like cage that could be rotated and reclined and generally adjusted into various positions. They used adolescent Jews because they wanted research-naïve subjects. Older Jews were more likely to have been used repeatedly in other experiments and were no longer considered reliable subjects for the fear and anxiety studies.

The subjects were given a choice of three different things to eat. The goal was to find a treat they liked more than any other. In most cases, they learned to choose the small piece of dark German chocolate. Once the food was determined, they were then required to reach over a shallow well on the table for the item.

Training could take a week or more for each step. The breeding program had produced Jews so fearful and anxiety-filled that every change to their environment was a deeply disturbing event.

Once a subject would consistently reach over the well for the treat, they were anesthetized and placed in the MRI and scanned. Then they were operated on and a select portion of their hippocampus was burned away with acid. When they recovered from the surgery they were fasted for three days to assure that they were hungry and motivated to perform. Then they again were seated at the table and had to reach across the well for the treat. This time, however, when the lid was pulled back, there was a snake in the well. In some experiments it would be a rubber snake, and at other times it would be a live bull snake.

The scientists watched to see whether or not the experimental brain damage affected the Jew's fear by measuring the time it took them to finally reach over the well for the treat. Some never would. Then they were killed. Their brains were sectioned and examined microscopically.

Drs. Ulrich Hamm and Frizt Kals had published some interesting papers about their discoveries.

The Germans had just left the room after taking blood from Levi and others. He looked over at the woman in the cell across from him again. She was thin, of slight build, and had black greasy dreadlocks. No one in the colonies was ever bathed except in preparation for surgery, and then, only the surgical site was scrubbed.

"Hey!" he said once again.

She looked over at him.

"At least tell me your name."

"Miriam."

"Finally!" he thought to himself. Levi pulled his mat to the front of the cell and sat down. "Miriam," he repeated. "That's a beautiful name. Where did you get it?" He hoped to coax her into some conversation.

She looked at him for some time. He thought she might not answer, but finally she did.

"I took it from a woman I knew and loved. She was taken and never came back. I was once called Ruth, but now I am Miriam."

"Miriam," he said again. "It is a beautiful name; she must have been a good friend."

Miriam looked at Levi for a long while without saying anything. Finally, "Were you born here?"

"No. I was six when they took us. I never saw my parents or my sisters again."

She stared at him. He thought she might be done talking.

"Tell me your story."

Levi was startled by her request. Asking to hear someone's story was the most intimate of questions in the colonies, one that invited and even demanded a bearing of the soul; it came with the implied promise to reciprocate. It carried with it a responsibility to always remember the story and to share it with others. Asking someone for their story was both a

16

demand and a commitment.

"You know what you're asking?"

"Yes. Perfectly," she answered. "I won't talk to you unless I really know you, and you really know me. Tell me your story."

Levi hadn't told his story in some time. It hurt. It wasn't the sort of thing he had shared often, even with the other nine. Telling them anything required telling it to the room, and no one told their story to anyone they couldn't see, assuming the person they were telling it to still could see. He sat and looked at her for a while. She seemed content to wait.

"You'll tell me yours?" he asked.

"I wouldn't have asked otherwise."

He took a deep breath and thought back for the first time in a very long time to his early years with his parents.

"OK."

Archie was sitting in his study after dinner reading the newspaper when he heard the car stop in front of the house. A moment later he heard his wife greeting his daughter, a little surprised that she had come over so late and unannounced.

"Cindy. Is everything all right?"

"Hi Mom. Yes, everything's fine. I dropped Rudy off at school; he's attending a guest lecture. He has a study session afterwards and will get a ride home. I was on the way home and just decided to stop. Is it ok?"

"Of course dear, you don't have to ask, this will always be your home too."

"Thanks Mom," she kissed her mother on the cheek. "I love you. Is Daddy in his study?"

"I'm in here!" came a shout. "Come in!"

"I'll make tea," said Trish.

Archie was sitting in an overstuffed oak-framed brocade armchair that had been in his family for three generations. Cindy walked in and gave her father a kiss and a hug. She sat down next to him in the chair's mate.

"Hi Daddy."

Archie put his paper aside. 'What's up?"

"Oh, nothing. Just thought I'd stop. How's work?"

"You didn't stop for nothing or just to visit. You didn't even look in the kitchen to see if there was pie. This must be serious."

She sighed. "Someone left a flyer in all the seats of my Modern Politics class two weeks ago. It caused quite a class discussion. My professor said it was all lies. Rudy has been asking around; some of the things it said might be true."

"What was in the flyer?" asked Archie.

"What flyer is that?" asked Trish coming in with a tray. There's no pie, but I made cookies this afternoon." She set a brightly flowered dessert plate of raisin oatmeal cookies and two cups of tea on the small lamp table between them and sat down with her own tea and cookie at a large messy desk.

"Cindy got some sort of literature at school that's bothering her," Archie said to his wife.

"Do you have it with you?"

"The pictures are horrible," she said. "I don't feel good about showing it to you."

"Let's see it honey," said her mother with concern.

Cindy reached into her bag and pulled out the flyer. She handed it to her father. "It's called Cruelty at RUC."

God's people endured. The not-so-young couple stood together in the dark corner of the warehouse as a few friends crowded in close together. A tiny candle was burning. The groom looked at his veiled bride and said as quietly as he could while being reasonably sure that everyone in the small gathering could hear him: "Behold, you are betrothed unto me with this ring, according to the law of Moses and Israel." The ring was a simple thin band of gold.

Everyone squeezed closer to hear Rebbe Shrinkle recite the sheva brachos, or seven blessings. A small glass of wine was passed among the group and finally to the couple who themselves shared the final sips. The serious risk of coming together had necessitated the abbreviation and modification of many ancient and holy ceremonies. A single glass was less risky than one for each guest. But not all tradition had been disposed of. The groom pulled out his handkerchief, wrapped it around the empty glass and set it on the floor. "Mazaltov! Mazaltov!" everyone whispered at the sound of the breaking glass.

In spite of themselves, everyone was smiling. They quietly circled the couple and placed small gifts and money into the groom's coat pocket. The newlyweds slipped away first. Rebbe Shrinkle and the guests hid his vestments and then they too slipped away and back into their personal worlds of guarded comments and hidden ancestry.

"Oh my God!" said Trish. "Who would print and say such things? This must have been written by Jews."

"Mother!" came Cindy's immediate reply. "Who cares who wrote it? Do you think these things are ok? I don't, and neither does Rudy. Look at that picture."

Trish looked at her husband and back at Cindy. "Didn't I hear you tell your father that one of your professors said it was all lies?"

Cindy looked at her father. "Do you think things like these are going on at the university?"

Archie took a sip of his tea. "A few scientists at the university use subhumans in their research. I don't know if they are doing things like this," he said, motioning to the brochure his wife was still holding and looking at. "There are regulations."

"We support medical research, Cindy," began her mother, "your father is a doctor after all. I'm sure the scientists do all they can to avoid hurting them. Some people are always against progress. And Jews have a history of lying."

Archie recalled one of the cases he worked on earlier in the day. A young black girl who was being used in studies of puberty had been exposed to large doses of testosterone early in her fetal development. She was born, like twenty-three other girls in the experiment, with deformed and masculinized genitals. Eight of the girls in the study had developed aggressive endometriosis and were in chronic pain. He had recommended euthanizing her but the principal scientist said that the data he could get from her before she died would be invaluable, so Archie had treated her pain as best he could.

"Daddy, does stuff like this go on at your hospital?"

Archie was in a quandary. His daughter was clearly distressed by the pamphlet. Although some of the claims it contained were not one hundred percent correct, enough of it was. The author's facts were generally accurate even if his or her opinions were extreme. He was afraid that the truth might make his daughter spurn him. He wanted her respect. Also, he had wrestled with his circumstances. If he quit, he might put his daughter's marriage in jeopardy, and he and his wife would be sure to lose stature and income. He didn't want to lie to his daughter, but he didn't want to lose her or risk her future either.

"A little maybe, but I don't know too much about it." The cookies sat uneaten on the pretty plate.

Tell Me Your Story

Levi Sach

"I remember my family and our house. I had an older brother and a younger sister, Donny and Debby. Donny was eight when they took us, Debby was four. I was six.

"We used to have big dinners, and I remember lots of people coming to our house. My mother made all sorts of delicious things to eat. My parents used to take turns reading to us at night. I remember a big blue book with bright pictures. One story was about a little woman who lived in a little house, everything she had was little. Another story was about goats who had to cross a bridge where a monster lived. I don't remember a lot about them now.

"My father used to recite poems to us that he said were very secret. I never understood them; they sounded funny.

"I remember my bed. It was so soft and warm. I had a box full of toys and things to play with.

"I remember going to school. I liked my teacher, Miss Simpson. She was tall and had red hair. We sang the Das Lied der Deutschen every morning. It went like this:

"Germany, Germany above all,
Above everything in the world,
When always, for protection,
We stand together as brothers.
From the Etsch to the Belt -
Germany, Germany above all
Above all in the world.

"I remember that I was playing *Uncle Wiggly* with my mom and dad and Debby when the door crashed open. The Germans rushed in with guns and were screaming at us. 'Jew! Jew!' they yelled. They were wearing helmets and masks. They were very big. My father jumped up and they shot him. My mother and my little sister were screaming. One of them grabbed me and dragged me out of the house and put me in the back of a van. I was screaming for my mother. I remember knowing when the van drove off that I wouldn't see any of them again.

"I was brought here. They took my clothes from me and said that subhumans don't need clothes. I was alone in a cell. I could hear lots of crying all around me, but I couldn't see anyone.

"I remember the first time they threw in food. I didn't know what it was. I was thirsty and didn't learn to use the lixit for a while. When I did, I felt like I could never get enough, even though the water tasted strange and was too warm.

"I remember wondering where I was supposed to go to the bathroom and being embarrassed when the Germans came and hosed out my cell. I tried to talk to them, but of course, they would say nothing to me. I just lay on the floor and cried.

"Eventually a German came and took me out of the cell. He seemed sort of friendly. He held my hand and led me to a room with two other men in it. They put me on a table and examined me. This was the first time they took samples from me. They cut out small parts of my skin, took blood, stuck a needle in my back and in my side. They held me down. Finally, they finished with me and put me in another cell. They never said a word.

"I learned to eat the kibble.

"They moved me to a room with other children, I could hear them and we tried to talk, but we were all very young. I could see two of them. They were very dirty and stared at me. I was very frightened.

"The Germans took us one at a time. They gave me a shot. When I woke up, I was strapped on hard board. A tube was in my arm, and another one was in my neck. I could see other children strapped down like me. Flat blue patches with wires attached to them were stuck on us. The wires went into a machine. Some of us were crying.

"They put something green in the tubes and it made us all start vomiting. Then they put something yellow in the tubes and most of the children started shaking and shaking. I think some died because they took them away. I didn't shake.

"Then they did it to us again. This went on for a long time. Finally, they took out the tubes and put me in another cell by myself.

"They didn't do anything to me for a long time. But one day, they took me again. They pulled out all the teeth on this side of my face." He pulled his mouth wide with his fingers to show Miriam as best as he could his bare eroded gums.

"After a while they dug holes in my gums and put in some kind of teeth. My mouth was swollen, and I had lots of stuff running out of my mouth. I couldn't eat. They pulled out those teeth, and put in others. They made me bite on things and put my head in machines. They did this over and over. There's a big hole now right here. Food is always stuck in it. It hurts all the time. Finally, they pulled out all the fake teeth and put me back in a cell.

21

Tell Me Your Story

"They didn't do anything to me for a long time. I was across from a man who couldn't hear. I thought maybe you couldn't hear either when they brought you. We could sort of talk. He used his hands to point to things and could make his hands seem like they were little people. There was something wrong with him and he used to shake all around his cell sometime. The Germans were making him swallow a pill every day.

Then one day, they took him away; I never had a name for him, and they brought in a woman. Her name was Wilhelmina. She told me her story.

She was nice to me and didn't seem to be hurt very badly. She taught me a lot about the colonies. She told me we were Jews. I knew I was a Jew, but she told me what it means to be a Jew. She told me that the Germans were really just regular people, and that real Germans wouldn't have to work at a place like this. She said they weren't allowed to talk to us because they didn't want us to learn to talk. She told me that we aren't as good as the Germans or even regular people because we are subhumans. The real Germans are the Master Race.

"The more I talked to her the more I was afraid and the more I hated them.

"Then one day they came again. And this time I was older and stronger and wouldn't come out. That's when I learned how strong they are. They pulled the lever and the back of the cage slid forward and pushed me against the front of the cage. They gave me a shot, and I woke up still in a new cell. I haven't seen Wilhelmina since then.

"They came every day and gave me another shot. I resisted for a long time. But my hands and arms and legs got bruised and twisted. The sliding wall was too strong. I quit fighting them, and one day they came and took blood instead of giving me a shot. Now they come and take blood from me every once in a while.

"Sometimes they take samples too, but they haven't done it in a long time. Then they brought you. That's my story."

Rudy had a 7:30 class on Monday mornings. Cindy's first class was at 9:00. They would go together and get Rudy a cup of coffee at Kaiser Union. He'd go on to class and Cindy would use the morning to study. As they came around the corner of Kelbling Hall, they were confronted by an already sizable crowd of students in front of the large gray limestone building.

"What's going on?" Rudy asked one of the students.

"I just got here too, I'm not too sure."

Campus Orpo, the Order Police, were in front of the building and putting yellow plastic ribbon across the entrance steps and keeping the students from entering. "Everyone should go to class! Disperse now!" ordered one of the officers. Obediently, the students started walking away in twos and threes. As the crowd thinned, Rudy and Cindy could see that the large glass doors had been broken.

On the wall between them someone had spray painted a message in bright red: "Frizt Kals is a murderer! Subhuman myth! HLF!"

"Move along! Go to class! Classes in this building are cancelled for today."

Major Klaus Waldschmidt was second in command of the RUC Orpo, the Ordnungspolizei. He was pacing again and wondering what to do. He had seen the pamphlet and a few others like it during his years at the university, but this was the first time anyone had resorted to vandalism. More vandalism could threaten his career. Oberst Schauenburg was retiring next year and Waldschmidt wanted the job. This was just the sort of problem that might make the administration look outside the RUC Orpo for the Oberst's replacement.

The student at the table seemed to be telling the truth, but she might still be hiding something. Helen Duppel was from a good German family. Her father was a well-respected member of the Korps der globalen Verwalter, and it was unlikely that she would have vandalized Kelbling Hall.

Major Waldschmidt sat down across from her at the small table once again. The room was bleak. An overhead lamp provided a searing illumination. A video camera in the corner of the ceiling kept a silent watch.

"Where did you get these?" he asked again. A small stack of brochures was on the table between them.

"I've told you already. They were on a table in my dorm's common room. Anyone could have left them there."

"But you were handing them out. Why were you doing that?"

"Again, Major Waldschmidt," she said with just a hint of haughtiness, "I read it and was shocked. I wanted my friends and other students to see it too. I knew if I left them there that one of the maids would just throw them away."

"What do you know about Kelbling Hall?"

"Why do you keep asking me that? I haven't done anything wrong. I don't know anything about it."

"If someone read that brochure and then vandalized the building, then it might be your fault because you gave it to them."

"But I don't even know who Fritz Kals is! There isn't anything about him in the brochure. Have you even read it?"

"Mind your manners Fräulein Duppel. My duty is to the World Reich, as is yours. Anything that challenges the smooth order of the government is a danger and an enemy of the Fatherland and the Master Race. Do not challenge me; I am a ranking officer in the Ordnungspolizei. We have notified your father that you are here and have ordered him to pick you up after this interrogation. I warn you again Fräulein. Any small thing you know and any small thing you are keeping hidden from me could be enough to send you to a detention and re-education center. You could bring great disgrace on your family."

"I've told you everything I know Herr Major. Did you have to call my parents?"

The following Saturday morning, Cindy came back to bed with two mugs of coffee and a plate of apple strudel. "So what did you find out?"

Rudy took a sip of the steaming coffee and a bite of the strudel. "I went to the library and did some searching. Kals has published a number of papers on fear."

"On fear?"

"Yes. The papers I read over claim that by studying the brains of Jews who are afraid, that they might be able to come up with a cure for shyness in German children."

"What? Shyness? That doesn't make any sense."

"They say that shyness is a serious problem for some German children."

"Weird. Why did they call him a murderer?"

"Well, after they study the Jews—they seem to have bred some to be afraid of just about everything—they kill them and look at parts of their brain with a microscope."

"You keep saying they."

"Yeah, there are two of them doing these experiments. Kals, who is a professor here, and Ulrich Hamm, the head of the psychiatry department at Joseph Mengele."

At mention of Joseph Mengele, Cindy stiffened. "But Daddy said there

24

wasn't anything going on with subhumans at the hospital."

"I know. You told me that. Here's another thing that I thought was odd. In one of the papers, Hamm and Kals say that the brains of Germans and subhumans are identical and that everything they learn from their experiments on Jews can be immediately applied to the Race. They don't seem to think there're any differences between Jews and Germans except that they can legally experiment on Jews. Maybe this has something to do with the quotation marks around subhuman in the pamphlet and the message on the wall at Kelbling."

"Let's bring this up at dinner tomorrow. I wonder if my father knows about this?"

Miriam

The Germans had been gone for a while. The lights had dimmed, but they were always on.

"Miriam," called Levi softly.

"What?" she was sitting in the back of her cell on her thin mat.

"You haven't told me your story. You owe me."

She sighed deeply and then dragged her mat to the front of the cell. "All right. I've been thinking about it; I want you to remember everything; I want to say it just right."

"I'll remember. I promise," whispered Rudy.

"Ok. I might have been born here. I don't remember any place else. Do you know what born means?"

"It means where you came from."

"Have you ever seen a baby? Do you know where babies come from?"

"A woman with a baby came to our house once. Where did she get it?

"Babies come out of women. I've had two babies. I'll tell you about them later. Your stomach starts to swell very slowly. There is a baby in you. After a while you can feel it moving inside you."

"Are you making this up? Having a baby inside you moving around sounds horrible. Did the Germans do that to you?"

"At first I didn't know what was happening, but I'll tell you about that when I get to it; I want to start at the beginning of my story.

"The earliest thing I can remember is the Germans hurting me. They put stuff on my back that burned me. They did it to me over and over again for a long time. Sometimes when I was locked up and I heard the door open, I would get so frightened that I would bite my arms really hard. I chewed off two of my fingers."

25

She held up her right hand and Levi saw that two fingers were bent stubs with dark purple scars. He had noticed the scars all over her.

"Another time, my food was different, it was awful tasting and every time I ate it my stomach would hurt."

"Is that when you felt the babies?" asked Levi.

"No, this has nothing to do with my babies. They came a long time later.

"Listen to my story. My shit was all runny, and I had blood coming out too. After a while I couldn't walk. I quit eating. They took me and took lots of samples and gave me injections, then they put me in another cell and I began getting regular food again. After a while I felt better.

"I started talking to people in other cells. They said things I didn't understand."

"I couldn't talk to people when I came here," said Levi. The words here are different; not everyone uses the same words."

"After a while, I began to understand more. I learned some things. They did something to my leg. They cut into me and when I awoke in my cell I had stitches in my hip. After that, my leg hurt all the time. It never stopped hurting. Sometimes they would hive me a shot and my leg wouldn't hurt so much; sometimes the injections didn't do anything and I would cry all night. Sometimes I cried all day too. My leg hurt for a long time.

"Then, they did surgery to me again and my leg got better. Even now, after a long time, I have to lay in a special way to keep it from aching all night. Can you see how it is different from my other leg now?" Miriam stood up.

Levy could see that one leg was thinner. The scar on her hip was a large one.

"After that they left me alone for a while. They took blood from me like they are doing to you, but they didn't hurt me much. I talked to the people who were around me in the rooms. I learned more. The Germans used me many times, but the experiments were not so bad as the first ones.

"One day, after examining me and taking samples, they put me in a cell with a man."

"You were in a cell with someone else?" Levi found this as amazing as the idea of babies crawling around inside someone.

"Yes. Listen. I was very afraid. For some reason the Germans didn't leave. They just stood there and watched us. The man grabbed me and knocked me to the floor. He did something to me. It's called fucking. His penis got bigger and he put it in me, here," she said touching her crotch.

Levi didn't know what to think of this. Miriam's story seemed to be getting more unbelievable. He couldn't imagine what she could be talking about. Sometimes his own penis got hard and bigger, so maybe that part was true, but what could she mean about putting it in her?

"The Germans were laughing and talking to each other. I heard the Germans talk many times while I was with the man. His name was Nathan. They liked to watch him fuck me. There were other men and women together in that room. The men fucked the women, and then a new woman was put in the cell. Nathan fucked me many times. After a while it didn't hurt as much.

"Then they put me in a new room. Everyone else in the room was a woman. We talked. All of them were fucked before they were brought to the women's room. This was the best room. We had more food. We had things to eat called fruit. It was better than food. It was wet and tasted different and very good.

"Some of the other women had swollen stomachs. Some of the women had already had babies before and told us that we all going to have a baby. They said we were pregnant. At first I didn't believe it, but my stomach started to swell and after a while I could feel the baby in me. I saw a baby come out of a woman. She was in the cell across from me. Her stomach was very big. She began moaning. Water was coming out of her. Some of the other women said she was going to have her baby; they told me to call out and tell them what was happening.

"I was very frightened because this was going to happen to me. It was the middle of the night. No Germans were around. She was on her back and put her feet against the bars, like this."

Miriam lay down and mimicked the woman's contortions. Levi was mesmerized. "After a long time, something started to happen and a small head started coming out."

"I don't understand," said Levi. "It came out of her?"

"It came out of the hole we were fucked in."

Levi looked again at Miriam's groin. There was a lot of hair. "Your shit hole?"

"No. Women have another hole. Look." Miriam pulled the hair away from her vagina. "Can you see? This where the baby comes out."

Miriam sat up again. "The baby came out and had something attached to its stomach, then something else came out, but I don't know what it was, it wasn't a baby, it came out of me too when I had my second baby. It must have scared the woman because she chewed it off her baby. The baby was crying and red. The woman held it to her breast, and it started sucking on her. They both fell asleep.

"The next morning the Germans took her and the baby away."

Tell Me Your Story

The lights suddenly brightened, and the sounds of the Germans coming back to work—the clashing of pans, doors opening and closing, muffled voices— made their stomachs tighten. They moved to the back of their cells again and hoped that the Germans would not come for them.

On Friday evening, Frizt Kals stopped in his driveway and took the mail out of the ornate wrought iron mailbox. The overhead door opened automatically and he pulled his black Audi into the garage. He went into the house and took the Jägermeister out of the freezer. He sat down at the kitchen table and looked over the mail. Of the four pieces, one seemed somewhat curious. It was hand-addressed to him, but it didn't have a return address. He wondered if it was from a past student. He put his finger under the flap and tore it open. As he slid his finger quickly along the top of the envelope, he felt a slicing pain. Blood spurted.

By Saturday afternoon, Orpo Major Waldschmidt was back in his office. He had heard from five scientists who had received similar envelopes booby-trapped with razor blades. Only Dr. Kals had actually been injured. Each envelope had contained a single sheet with the same hand printed message: "You have been targeted, and you have 10 days to announce in public that you have stopped your 'subhuman' experiments. If you do not heed our warning, your violence will be turned back on you."

His phone rang. It was Orpo Hauptmann Helmut Arendt, head of security at Joseph Mengele Memorial Hospital for Genetic and Racial Disease. "Heil Hitler! Major Waldschmidt. A situation has arisen here, and I would like the advice of a senior officer."

"What is it, Hauptmann Arendt? I am very busy."

"Yes, Herr Major; only a moment. A scientist and our subhuman colony doctor received booby-trapped envelopes in the mail last night. They had razor blades hidden inside. They contained notes threatening them. I'm only asking because I know that there was vandalism on your campus last week that might be related to this."

They heard the last door close. The lights dimmed. The colony rooms began to fill with soft chatter as people began visiting with each other once again. There were thirty cells in most rooms, facing each other from each side of a gray hallway. Concrete walls separated the cells. The steel-bar front wall of each cell was set back a meter from the end of the walls separating the cells making the it nearly impossible to see into the cells on either side of the one directly opposite.

The cells were stark and barren. A lixit, a stainless steel tube that provided a miserly supply of tepid water, a thin foam mat, and one other item completed each cell's appointments. The other items were either a brightly colored plastic ball, a small stainless steel mirror attached to the front of the cage, or a small knobby piece of hard rubber. Periodically, the items were switched from cell to cell by the Germans. It was called psychological enrichment.

At the far back of the cell, where the concrete floor met the concrete wall— on the other side of the moveable back wall of bars—there was a shallow trough running from cell to cell the length of the room. When the Germans hosed down a cell, the water and wastes were washed into the trough and out of the room. The Germans always started at one end of a room with the hose. By the time they had worked their way to the other end, the feces and uneaten kibble had sometimes accumulated into a large waterlogged mass. The subjects in the cells at the lower end were subjected to significantly more harassment because the Germans stood in front of those cells for a longer time with their high-pressure hose.

Trish was setting the brisket on the table when Cindy and Rudy came in the front door.

"I'm so sorry we're late Mom," said Cindy. "The traffic was unbelievable on Der Führer Strasse."

"We're just glad you are both here. Get washed up and let's all sit down. Honey!" she called, "Cindy and Rudy are here. Mary, dinner's ready!"

When the family was around the table, Archie asked Mary to say grace.

"Dear Lord, thank you for the food we are about to eat and for all the wonderful things you have given us. Thank you for my family. Thank you for my teacher and friends. Please don't let the extremists hurt Daddy. Thank you for our wonderful World Reich. Thank you for everything Lord. Heil Hitler. Amen."

"Heil Hitler. Amen," repeated the family.

"Who's trying to hurt you?" Cindy asked looking at her father. "What extremists?"

Before he could answer, Trish got up and walked over to the large pine hutch. "Look at this," she said. "Those people sent a razor blade to your father. To your father! He might have been seriously hurt. We heard that a doctor at the university got one too and sliced a finger so badly that he might not be able to do any surgery again." She handed the letter to her daughter. "This is just a copy. The Orpo took the original for analysis."

"Now honey," said Archie. "Can't this wait until after dinner? Mary, where'd you hear anything about extremists?"

"Mother says those people are bad. She said they're extremists, didn't you Mom? She said they might even be Jews."

Cindy and Rudy looked at each other. He squeezed her hand under the table. "Daddy, we've heard that Ulrich Hamm and Frizt Kals are doing horrible experiments on subhumans. Kals teaches at the university. He's the one whose finger was cut. Does Hamm work at your hospital? Does he really experiment on their brains and frighten them?"

Archie thought back to what Orpo Hauptmann Helmut Arendt, head of security at Joseph Mengele had told him over the phone after Dr. Nelson had called in about the envelope. He had considered it mildly ironic or a little suspicious that only a day earlier he had worked with Dr. Hamm in an attempt to increase the survival rate of his subjects. Hamm and Kals had branched out from their focus on the amygdala, and now were lifting the whole brain to give them access to the ventral surface. They were suctioning away parts of the orbitofrontal cortex. Some of the subjects died from hemorrhages and others, though they survived the highly invasive surgeries, were severely impaired. He had been working with Hamm to improve his pre- and post-operative medications. Dr. Nelson thought that if the swelling could be prevented that more of them would survive and might be less impaired.

Archie had these recollections in a moment's time; he wondered yet again what he should tell his family.

"Can you believe they sent a death threat to your father?" said Trish with a tone of moral outrage. "Of all people. Isn't this just like the Jews? First that nasty brochure you brought over—I hope you are seeing that you can't trust anything these people say—and now these lies about your father. Your father isn't even a scientist; he's a doctor! They don't know what they are talking about. Pass the green beans to your father, Mary."

Cindy watched her father. She hadn't taken her eyes from him since asking about Hamm. There was something about the way he looked at her mother, the way he was sitting, she wasn't sure just what, but he seemed conflicted.

"What is it Daddy? You seem upset or something."

"Of course he's upset Cindy. Who wouldn't be? Terrorists threatened him today. I'm frightened too."

Archie shot his wife a glance and said to his younger daughter, "Your mother is going overboard about this Mary. There isn't anything to be worried about. It's probably just kids playing pranks."

"I don't know, Dr. Nelson," said Rudy. "The damage on campus was more than a prank. These people, whoever they are—they may not be Jews," he looked over at Cindy, "but they seem serious to me. Do you know Dr. Hamm or Dr. Kals?"

There it was. He knew he wasn't going to be able to sidestep the matter any longer. He looked down at the meat on his plate. For some reason, he saw it in anatomical terms rather than culinary. His wife had been buying better cuts since they gained access to the exclusive Master Race grocery stores, but she continued to buy the occasional brisket. He had encouraged her because, in spite of its somewhat coarse texture, her slow cook recipe and repeated basting made it one of her most delicious meals. Her recipe had been in the family for a long time. But now, as he looked at the meat on his plate, he could see only the muscle, the deep pectoral muscle that he knew had been attached to the *supraspinatus*.

"Daddy?" Cindy said, reviving him from his revere.

"Yes. Of course. Mary, go to your room. Take your plate and milk with you."

"What did I do?" came the immediate protest. "Why do I have to go to my room?"

"This is an adult conversation. You don't need to be here."

"Mom!" came her appeal.

Archie looked at his wife. She read the seriousness in his eyes. She stood and helped Mary with her plate. "Oh honey, this is just boring adult stuff. You can watch that new video."

When Trish came back a dark mood hovered around the table. No one was eating. "So what's all this drama for?"

"I was just beginning to tell the kids about my job. I haven't really talked to you about it either. It's not what you think."

Archie told them about his job as the colony doctor. He explained that he didn't like it and disagreed with some of the decisions that were made, but that he felt he was doing some good by trying to alleviate as much suffering as he could. The last few colony doctors had let things go and the quality of medical and daily care for the subjects had deteriorated. He was working to make things a little better for them.

When he finished talking, no one said anything. Cindy was stunned; Rudy could sense her confused emotions.

Trish put a forkful of the brisket in her mouth and began chewing slowly. Cindy thought about the damage to the building on campus and the scrawled message on its wall. She looked down at the copy of the threat letter that was still lying on the table between her and Rudy. She got up from the table and went over to her purse. She came back with the brochure and set it on top of the threat. "How much of this is true, Daddy?"

"Cindy!" Her mother reacted immediately to defend her husband. "How dare you! Your father is a good man he wouldn't do any of those things, even to Jews or niggers."

Archie reached across the table and picked up the brochure. He opened it up and put his finger on one paragraph. "Well, here it says that scleral search coils are glued to eyelids. Actually, they are sutured directly to the eye. And here, it says that there are a thousand subhumans on campus. I don't know the exact number, but I think it must be less than a hundred. We send the university more subjects when they need them, but most university researchers come to Mengele and use our labs. We have 7,831 subjects on hand right now. The rest of the brochure is pretty accurate as far as it goes. I know how this sounds, but ..."

"You said that nothing like this was going on," said Cindy.

"I just wanted to protect you. This is a complex and complicated part of science. I knew you would be mad at me if you found out what I really do."

"I'm sure your father is doing what's right Cindy," said her mother.

"Why are you involved in this Daddy? This isn't right."

"Cindy, there are implications for all of us. I couldn't turn down the job."

"Why not?"

"Non-Aryans with daughters marrying into the Master Race don't dare do such things. Your future, even Mary's future and your mother's security depend on me being a good and obedient servant."

Cindy looked at Rudy. "Rudy wouldn't do anything if you refused the job or if you quit. Would you?"

"Dr. Nelson, I hope you know how much I love your daughter and how fond I've become of all of you. I feel like a part of the family. I would never do anything to harm or cause any of you to be hurt in any way. Just so you know sir, I do not agree with what is being done to these people in the name of German science. This is an abomination."

"I can't believe you're involved in all of this because of me," said Cindy. The tears were just beginning to fill her eyes. "I want you to stop, Daddy."

"Honey, I really appreciate everything Rudy said and admire your strong feelings, but you don't really understand the situation. I can't quit; we have to make as much good out of this as we can."

"I want to go home Rudy."

Miriam

She pulled her mat to the front of her cell. Levi was already sitting in the front of his cell. His face was pressed against the steel bars.

"One day, right after they had hosed the cells," she said, "I started getting strong pains. My stomach was large. Other women said my baby was coming. I was very afraid. I couldn't stand up. I started crying out because it hurt so much. The Germans took me to a small room and put me on a table. They pushed on my stomach and looked between my legs. I think they might have put something in me, but I was screaming, the pain was so bad I don't know what happened. They gave me a shot.

"I woke up in a new room. At first, I thought I was back in the women's room, but I could hear cries that were different. The Germans came to my cell and gave me a baby. It was crying. I knew it was my baby. I didn't know what to do with it, but I remembered the woman across from me and how her baby sucked on her, so I held my baby close and it stopped crying and began sucking my breast. The Germans watched for a while and then left.

"This wasn't a good room. The Germans came often and took our babies. We all fought them. When they brought the babies back, they were different. Then after a while they took them again and when the brought them back they were very bad. They stayed rolled in a ball and cried out when we touched them. They would suck, but then they would roll up again.

"The Germans took them many times. I called my baby Little Jen. One day they never brought the babies back. They took me and took samples. Then they put me in a regular room.

They didn't do anything to me for a while. They started taking my blood again. Then they took me back to the fuck room. I was in with a man who couldn't talk and was very rough. They finally moved me back to the women's room and I knew I was going to have another baby.

Fritz Kals' right index finger still hurt. It still throbbed at night even after two weeks. The slice had been deep and had severed a tendon. Surgeons had repaired it, but he worried about the fine motor skills. He was scheduled to begin rehabilitation in a week.

He left his office and rode the elevator down to the basement garage. He got in his black Audi, turned the key in the ignition and detonated the small pipe bomb that had been hidden beneath his seat. As he was bleeding to death, he noticed that his finger no longer hurt.

North American Oberstgruppenführer Heinz Schimmelpfennig was at the head of the table. He hadn't said much and was content, for the moment, to listen to his officers' plans and ideas. The Orpo, the Order Police, kept order around the world. Political movements were rarely tolerated; those that were allowed to exist professed a strong allegiance to the World Reich and the Race. All political movements had to be licensed.

Orpo Hauptmann Helmut Arendt, assistant head of security at Joseph Mengele Memorial Hospital for Genetic and Racial Disease was saying that he did not have enough officers to provide adequate security for every scientist at the hospital.

Major Klaus Waldschmidt was saying that the university didn't have adequate manpower either.

Hundreds of additional brochures had been found around the campus. Every car in a parking lot for the non-Aryan staff of the hospital had a brochure stuck on the windshield. Five more researchers had received threat letters. All the staff, Master Race and others, were worried and on edge.

Both men felt that a strong showing of force was needed right away. They admitted to Schimmelpfennig that they had no real leads. He looked at the two men and the other Ordnungspolizei at the table and around the room. He swelled with pride at their intelligence, dedication, and perfect adherence to duty. He was proud to be their leader and even more proud of the Race and the Fatherland.

Rick Bogle

The Second Part

Rudy took his final swallow of coffee and headed toward the front door. "Let's go. We're already ten minutes late."

"And whose fault is that?" asked Cindy with a deadpan look at her husband as she walked to the door with her book bag and purse.

Rudy grabbed her with a hint of roughness as if to admonish her. He buried his head in her hair and said, "It's all your fault. All yours. I can't resist you."

Rudy pulled away after one more long kiss and said, "Let's get out of here."

They hurried out but stopped short. A uniformed Orpo officer was standing next to their door.

"What's going on?" demanded Rudy.

The policeman snapped to attention and introduced himself. He explained that his orders were to guard their door and to detain any non-Aryan visitors for possible interrogation.

Cindy began questioning the young man, but Rudy said it wouldn't do any good. They hurried to the elevator. When the door opened in the lobby, they saw another officer, and even another at the building's front door. Most disconcerting were the two plain clothed young men who introduced themselves as Sicherheitspolizei officers assigned to follow them and provide security when they weren't at home. The SiPo were described on television and in the papers as the Reich's most elite security forces.

The World Reich had more than a million police. Many garrisons were maintained in every Zustände. Dissent anywhere was quelled quickly and decisively. Leaders were identified and arrested. Large numbers of Orpo could be called quickly into service anywhere at any time.

The order from North American Oberstgruppenführer Heinz Schimmelpfennig was immediately obeyed. Within 48 hours ten thousand new security officers, both Orpo and SiPo were on duty in Chicago. They were guarding all the research staff of both Joseph Mengele Memorial Hospital for Genetic and Racial Disease and Reich University. Others were infiltrating the student body, the research staff, asking questions, and investigating every lead.

Miriam

The lights dimmed and Miriam continued her story. "The women's room is a good place. I was glad to be back, but I was afraid too because I knew I had another baby coming. All I could do was worry. I began chewing my hand again.

"A new woman was put in the cell across from me. She told me to stop biting myself. Her name was Miriam." Miriam stopped talking and put her head against the bars. Levi wished he could touch her. This confused him; he had never wanted to touch anyone and hated the Germans touching him.

Miriam looked up at him. "You remind me of her right now. She used to look at me like you are doing."

Rebbe Shrinkle stepped out of his office building and into the street. He headed down the block and was joined by another man who was browsing a newsstand.

"Well hello Jim, how are you doing?"

"Just fine Fred, how are you?"

They shook hands and began walking together down the street. Rebbe Shrinkle was James Peterson in public. His small congregation was careful about what they said and where they said it, but they needed to ask him for advice at times. They walked along and spoke quietly to each other.

"I work at the hospital. New police are everywhere. We have new employees. The university is saying that Jewish extremists are responsible for everything."

"Be friendly but don't make new friends."

"Everyone is being looked at carefully. My papers are good but my wife is missing the certificate for her grandmother. This hasn't ever been a problem, but so many police are looking for Jews right now."

"Papers can be lost. You are a good citizen. Say nothing. Don't act surprised. Be matter of fact. Stay away from us for a while. God bless you."

Rebbe Shrinkle crossed the street alone.

Rudy was sitting at a table in the Rathskeller, the beer garden in the student union, with two of his friends. At the door some distance away, his SiPo shadow sat with two other SiPo plainclothesmen. Rudy and his friends were drinking from a pitcher of Kölsch. One of them asked, "So. Any new students in any of your classes?"

"We have a new TA in my history class. There's a new student in my philosophy class. How about you guys?"

They laughed for a while about the obvious spies among them. Rudy mentioned his shadow waiting at the door. Stephen, a tall blond boy, said with some earnesty, "I've heard that they are trying to find the leaders. In my biology class, two Orpos come with Dr. Shlenk when he lectures. There are cops everywhere.

"They'll never find them," said Phillip.

"Why do you say that? The Orpo always win. When haven't they?"

"There are no leaders."

"What does that mean. You're a damn Gypsy."

The boys finished the pitcher and picked up their books. Rudy held back after Stephan had headed off and asked Phillip, "Do you think they'll keep the pressure on?"

"The Orpo?"

"The bombers."

"What do you think?"

Both were cautious. They looked at each other for a moment. "I hope they make the university stop what its doing."

"Let's talk more on Wednesday."

Archie disliked some parts of his job at Mengele more than others. He took off his clothes and donned a blue paper jumper. Two technicians helped him step into the full-body suit. Once in, they zipped up the back of the suit and pulled the rubber seal over the zipper. They helped him put on the clear plastic helmet and attach the air hose to the port. He always felt like a Greek sponge diver when they hooked the hose to him.

The techs stepped back and he felt the pressure in the suit increase slightly. After five minutes, the seals in his suit were judged secure and he was disconnected. They handed him the end of the hose. He didn't mind this part too much.

He walked to a door that looked like a submarine hatch and stepped over the high threshold. One of the technicians closed and sealed the hatch behind him. As he walked to the hatch on the other side of the small airlock the air pressure increased automatically. The hatch opened, and Archie stepped into the hospital's extreme biohazard lab, or EBL. As the hospital's colony doctor he was required to make an annual inspection of all the labs using subhumans. The EBL was one of the labs that he wished he did not have to visit, ever.

The subjects brought here never left; that wasn't quite true, he thought to himself, actually they did leave, as smoke from the incinerator. The lab was always busy; the waiting list was at least a year long he had heard. Most of the research conducted at the lab was military and Orpo ordered. The large majority of the scientists who used the lab were visiting from Germany or Austria; they wanted to use subhumans, but importation of subhumans into the Fatherland was banned, as were laboratories that studied the world's most deadly diseases.

Currently, two visiting scientists were studying the 1918 Spanish flu. In a little under a year, the disease killed between 20 and 100 million people worldwide. It had been extinct until Drs. Kurt and Karl Eisendorf used old American and Canadian documents to locate the bodies of Spanish flu victims who had been buried in the permafrost. The Eisendorfs were able to extract enough of the virus's RNA to be able to piece back together its entire small genetic code.

Since doing so, they had been infecting subhumans with the virus and documenting the course of the invariably fatal disease. They had been at the EBL for almost a month this time and were leaving in a few days. Everyone in the EBL was dressed like Archie and had their air hoses attached to valves near their workstations. Most of the workers were bent over microscopes.

There were six small cells in the room. The door of one was opened and two workers were inside and rolling a corpse onto a gurney. It was a man. His face and chest were caked in coagulated blood and mucus. In the next cell, a woman was lying on a thin mat and obviously struggling to breathe;

bloody mucus was bubbling from her nose and mouth. Archie knew the course of the disease and expected that she would be dead within a few hours. She was comatose, fortunately for her.

The subject in the next cell was just beginning to cough up blood clots.

In the three cells across the aisle, apparently healthy subjects sat huddled against the back walls.

"Ah! Dr. Nelson," came a muffled voice from one of the figures that had just looked up from a microscope. "Karl, Dr. Nelson is here to inspect our subhumans' accommodations."

A figure next to him looked up. "Dr. Nelson, how have you been?"

"Fine. Thank you for asking. Have you been providing the blankets I asked you to give to the subjects when the chills begin? I don't see any in the cells."

"We certainly tried, didn't we Karl?"

"Ja. But the blankets became filthy; the large volume of expectorant you know, and really, the chills are not a result of the air temperature, as you well know Dr. Nelson. They receive very little comfort from such things."

Archie knew that arguing with visiting German scientists was a pointless exercise; all he could do was to include their deviation from his recommendation in his report; he knew that nothing would be done; they were scheduled to leave the lab at the end of the week and would return to Germany.

Archie finished his inspection and then began the long decontamination process.

North American Oberstgruppenführer Heinz Schimmelpfennig was a little disappointed. After a full month of careful and exhaustive investigation, the only new fact that had come to light was that the brochures had been printed on copiers in Kaiser Union. So many different students used the union copiers so often that this discovery was of very little practical value. The investigation had stalled.

"No one seems to know anything, Oberstgruppenführer. We have agents in every department now, and in most classes and in most clubs. We have phone taps, email taps, we have bugs in all the dormitories; no one is talking."

"What about that student, the girl caught handing them out?"

"She is telling the truth. I am certain of it, Oberstgruppenführer. If she was lying, we would have found out by now."

"But how can people write brochures, mail threats, put bombs in cars, and no one knows anything about it?"

"Maybe, Oberstgruppenführer, the same person did everything? Maybe not, and no one knows each other?"

The Orpo officers sitting around the table considered these possibilities. "We must find the leaders," said one of them. "We must work harder." They all nodded in agreement.

Rudy and Phillip were in the same economics class, "Microeconomics of Zustände Export Businesses." They were sitting at a library table studying for an exam and quietly asking each other review questions. A few tables down, Rudy's SiPo shadow sat reading a magazine.

Rudy knocked a book and a pen off the table with his elbow. The pen rolled under the table. He picked up the book and had to get out of his chair to retrieve the pen. As he did so, he also looked at the underside of the table and then took his seat again.

"It's ok," he said quietly.

"Last week I spotted a small microphone under a table at the Kaiser," said Phillip. "They're listening to everything now."

"We want to help," said Rudy.

"I only know one other person," said Philip. "And now you. This is very dangerous."

"What can we do?"

"That's up to you," explained Phillip. "Everyone does what they can. No one knows everyone else. I don't know who did the bomb; I don't know who did the letters."

"Did you do the brochure?"

"We can't and shouldn't ask each other too many questions, but yes, I helped. My friend has ways of learning what's happening in the labs. We have to get the word out."

"What you are doing is important. We wouldn't have known, no one would have known what's really going on. It's all so horrible and unbelievable."

"It isn't unbelievable. What do you know about the war?"

"What do you mean? I know a lot. I love history."

"About the Jews and the death camps, about the secret experiments."

"I know that the Jews were exterminated in Europe, but I haven't heard anything about secret experiments. I read that the extermination was done humanely and had to be done to protect the purity of the Race," said Rudy, repeating his history lessons.

"There was nothing humane about the extermination. I'll try to get you something to read. I hope you decide to get active, but whatever you do, you must be absolutely careful. Whatever you do, never tell anyone, even me. I don't know why I admitted to the brochure. That was stupid."

Miriam

"I began chewing on my arms again when I felt my stomach getting bigger. I remembered Little Jen and how I felt when they took her away. I remembered how she was when they brought her back.

"The Germans sometimes put something wet on my arms and once put something around my neck that made it hard for me to put my hands in my mouth, but I couldn't eat and they took it off.

"Then, one day, they put Miriam in the cell across from me. She was older. She began talking to me almost as soon as the Germans were gone. It took me a while to understand her; she used lots of words I didn't know. Every time I put my arm in my mouth she told me to stop.

"She said that she had been a secretary. She tried to tell me what that means, but I never understood. She told me we were Jews and that the Germans hate Jews. She said that she had a family, but that now they were all dead or in labs. She said she was being punished and would be killed.

"She told me that once, a long time ago, Jews weren't in labs; she said that Jews and everyone else used to be free.

"She told me about something called Outside. She said that the floor is soft and green outside. She said that the ceiling is blue and sometimes things called clouds, big white things slide across it. She called the floor the grass, and the ceiling the sky. She talked about things called flowers and chocolate and so many other beautiful things. She told me about things called animals and would sometimes laugh and laugh when she told me about someone called Buddy. Buddy was an animal; she called him a dog. Animals can't talk, she said, but they lick you and love you and play with you.

"Miriam told me about her family and what it was like to have a family and to be in love. I told her I had been with two men, but she said that wasn't love. She called it rape.

"Everything I know about the real world I learned from Miriam. She used to call me Sweetie, and said I was a child and that she loved me too.

41

She said I was like her daughter.

"We talked everyday. I learned so much. It makes me sad to dream of Outside. I miss Miriam everyday.

"One day, they came for her. It was different. Many men came, some were wearing funny clothes and had shiny things sort of like the Germans use in the experiments, but these were on their clothes. They were yelling at her and she was yelling back. She fought with them. They didn't use the squeeze bars with her. They didn't give her a shot; they dragged her out. She yelled to me, "Tell everyone. I love you. Don't forget me."

"That was the day I became Miriam."

It was a Sunday afternoon. Sprinklers were tick, tick, ticking circular paths of water in the manicured suburban yards. Rudy was at the library studying for finals. Trish and her younger daughter were shopping for dinner. Archie and Cindy were sharing an old and creaking porch swing on the back deck. Archie was sipping an iced tea after mowing the lawn; a slice of lemon floated in the perspiring glass.

"You guys will be done with school soon," he said.

"We can't wait," said Cindy. She wasn't sure how to broach the subject again with her father. "How's work Daddy?"

"Do we really want to go there?"

Cindy laid her head against her father's shoulder. He smelled of sweat and soap. "I know you Daddy. You always taught us to be kind. I don't believe you are happy at work."

"Sit up," he said. "We've talked about this already. You know there isn't anything I can do. There's no sense in discussing it. Try to put it all out of you mind."

"I don't think we can do that. Rudy and I don't like what's going on. We want to do something."

"I've told you, damn it. There isn't anything. Forget about it."

"We think there might be something, Daddy." Cindy ignored his cursing. He never cursed. His strong words reinforced her opinion that he was troubled by the things he was doing. "We have a plan; but it depends on you."

Archie stood up and walked to the steps leading to the lawn. He sat down and looked at his watch. He looked up at the sky and noticed a single darkening cloud. Maybe there would be a shower later in the day.

"Your mother and sister will be home soon. What's your plan?"

Rebbe Shrinkle sat on a park bench watching his son and other children playing on bright red and green playground equipment. He had a newspaper with him. A man and a woman holding a young girl's hand walked up and stopped in front of the bench. The woman told the girl to go play. "Do you mind if we sit here?" asked the man.

"No, of course not," answered the Rebbe. He knew the man; Henry was part of the Rebbe's small congregation. The meeting had been arranged with infinite care and circumspection over a month's time. The risk for all of them was great but they were putting many others at grave risk as well.

They sat watching the children for a while, Henry and the woman sitting together a little distance on the bench from the Rebbe. An observer would not easily recognize that the three of them were meeting. Finally, the woman said to no one in particular, "Thank you for agreeing to help us Rebbe."

Rebbe Shrinkle opened his paper to the editorial page and said softly, "I've made arrangements. When I leave, I'll leave my paper behind. Don't pick it up right away. You'll find a name and address penciled in the classifieds. It's in Chicago of course. They can't take more than six; even six will be hard. You must meet with them soon to arrange details. I can't do more than this." He folded his paper and set it on the bench between them and stood up. "Benny!" he called, "Let's go." A little boy ran to him and took his hand as they walked away.

Miriam

"When my second baby came, the German's left him with me for a while. I called him Nick. Miriam told me that she had a son named Nick, so I named my baby Nick too.

"They moved us to a different room. The room was filled with other women and babies. I couldn't see them, but I could hear them crying sometimes and making the little sounds that babies make. They gave us fruit. It wasn't a bad room, but the Germans took some of the babies and the mothers always fought, so it wasn't as good as the women's room.

"I loved Nick more than Little Jen. I didn't really know her; they hurt her when she was so little and took her away so soon. Nick used to look at me and smile sometimes. He would hold my fingers and snuggle close

43

to me at night. But they took him. I knew they would. What could I do?"

Levi had never cared too much about anything other than his food and avoiding the German's rough treatment. But Miriam was different than any of the others he had known. She was different from everything in his bleak life. He wanted to touch her, to put his arms around her, he cried sometimes when she was telling her story; he was confused by her and the feelings he had.

"You couldn't do anything," he said. "The Germans are too strong."

Archie had gone over the problem for many days, but the solution had appeared on it's own. He had promised to try to get a pass card for Cindy and Rudy. That was to be his sole part in their crazy plan. He had argued with them about it; he had pointed out the risks, the dangers, the possible problems, but in the end, he had agreed to help them; the reality of the lab had invaded his dreams. But getting a card that would open all the doors was harder than he had imagined it would be, and, in fact, he had all but given up when it happened at the end of the day on a Friday.

Mengele had a full locker room and showers. All the colony workers showered before and after their day's work. It reduced the chance of introducing pathogens into the colony and allowed them to wash off the stench before going home.

The lab had hired two new colony workers. The men had been on the job only a few days and were still confused about the routine. Archie put his lab coat and scrubs into the large laundry hamper before taking his shower. He walked to the shower entrance and into the thick fog of steam coming from the open passageway. Wooden pegs stuck out of the wall; towels hung on some of them. Trousers hung on one. He knew immediately that one of the new men had hung them there rather than putting them in a locker. He hesitated for a moment fearful that someone would come out and find him going through the man's pants. He would just tell them that he was looking for the owner's name if they did. But he felt the pass card almost immediately in a front pocket. The neck chain was wound around it. He hoped that the new man would think that he had misplaced the card and postpone reporting it. Archie thought the man might be fired if he did report it and hoped the man realized that as well. Since the man—John F. Bowden said the name on the card—would be working with others for sometime before being allowed to work alone, he wouldn't necessarily need his card anyway, he might be able to get along without it for some time. Archie hoped he would try to hold on to his new job for a while.

And then, standing naked in the steam, holding the card in his hand, Archie almost panicked. He had been so careful lately and had begun seeing the many small security cameras in the halls and in the colony rooms; they seemed to be everywhere once he took notice of them. He was sure that there would be at least one in the locker room; he couldn't go back to his locker with the card in his hand. Just a moment later he was in the shower with empty hands and clenched buttocks.

Rudy and Cindy were standing shoulder to shoulder on the West Lake Street Bridge overlooking the confluence of the north and west branch of the Chicago River. On Phillip's suggestion, they had stopped talking in their apartment about the subhuman activism and problems on campus.

"Are you sure you want to go ahead with this?" asked Rudy. "It's not too late to stop the whole thing."

"Do you want to stop it?" she asked, turning and looking into his eyes.

"No. I'm just sick with worry. If anything goes wrong, you and your father could go to jail for a long time, maybe worse. Your family would be dishonored for a generation."

"You're taking the same risk." They stood quietly as a train on the Lake Street L passed loudly overhead. A glimmering white tourist boat turned lazily in the basin below them.

When the train passed, Rudy said, "You know that's not true. I'd be an embarrassment to my parents, maybe, but I haven't talked to them about any of this and don't know how they would feel about it. I'd lose my scholarship and might get deported, but it's unlikely that anything harsh would be done to me; it would be blamed on your father and your influence. They'd say I was just a victim of lower race schemes to damage the Reich and the Race."

"Well, who's going to do this if we aren't? This is a chance to really make a difference. I understand the risk. I know we can do this."

Rudy pulled her closer to him, "If I lost you, I'd kill myself. You're right though, with the pass card we should be able to get in and out easily. I love you so much. Let's go over the details one more time."

Tell Me Your Story

Phillip had found himself at the hub of a plan that involved almost a dozen people, most of whom he hadn't met and who had no specific knowledge of each other. Every step of the way was filled with opportunities for failure; at least no one could identify everyone else. If things went sour, maybe some of them wouldn't be caught.

"If things worked out," he mused to himself, "things might get really crazy."

Finals at RUC were finally over. Couches, mattresses, old bicycles, dented empty beer kegs, and sundry other items lined the streets in the surrounding rental neighborhoods as students cleaned out their apartments and got ready to go home over the summer. The campus was deserted. The student union and the library were quiet and empty for the first time in months.

Three bombs were timed to explode in sequence, and they worked perfectly. The first went off at 7 PM in a bathroom at the Rathskeller. The Orpo were already on the scene when the fire department arrived. It had been a big bomb; it blew out the floor above it and the wall next to it. A gas line had been sheared and the fire had grown quickly. The firemen called in a second alarm as soon as they arrived.

Exactly an hour later, the bomb in the library detonated. Unlike the bomb in Kaiser Union, the bomb in the library was actually designed to start a fire. It exploded into a ball of flame and propellant and sparked a fire that spread rapidly. The sprinkler system came on immediately, but the water pressure was low because many hoses were already pouring water onto the flames at Kaiser.

Orpo responded quickly, but fire trucks were later in arriving. The library fire looked as if it might be an even bigger problem than the union fire.

Across town at Mengele, Rudy, Cindy, and Phillip were sitting in a van in a parking ramp at the hospital. They each had a bag of gear and were dressed in uniform black hooded sweatshirts and jeans. They wore the same shoes. Black balaclavas were rolled into caps on their heads.

There were a few other cars parked around them, but the ramp was mostly empty. They were parked near the back entrance used by the colony staff. They knew, from the plans that Archie had drawn for them that the door opened on to a short hallway that led to the locker room. They were tense and kept looking at their watches. They thought they might have heard the first bomb explode but they hadn't heard the second. They were somewhat encouraged by the sounds of the many police and fire sirens that were passing the hospital.

Cindy looked at her watch again and said, "Let's go."

Major Klaus Waldschmidt was acting commander of the RUC Orpo now that Oberst Schauenburg had taken an early retirement. He was observing the firefighters' efficient battle against the flames at the union when the library bomb exploded. He took the time to drive to the library and survey the situation first hand. The response was taking too long, but he recognized the strain on the fire department's resources. When he saw the fire he was certain that it had been another bomb. He called Oberstgruppenführer Heinz Schimmelpfennig who arrived on the scene quickly.

The Fire Marshal was with the two men in a mobile command station that had been activated right after the second fire erupted. Already, fire engines and fire fighters from across the city had been summoned. Nearby towns had alerted their own staff; the entire area was on standby to cover the more pedestrian calls that were bound to keep coming in, in spite of the conflagration on campus demanding so many resources.

Just as the third bomb exploded—this one at the university's main steam plant, igniting a 92-ton heap of powdered bituminous coal—Rudy swiped John F. Bowden's pass card.

The sirens woke Archie. His wife was almost snoring next to him; she'd always been able to sleep through anything. He lay quietly, but when the sirens didn't stop and seemed to grow in number, he got out of bed and went downstairs and clicked on the television. Multiple fires on Reich University campus the news was blasting.

Levi had heard the sounds before, but this time they seemed to just go on and on. He also thought he heard doors opening somewhere, but the Germans were all gone. The whole room was up and talking about it. Then, much louder than the high wailing distant noises, came a ringing and blaring from within the building at the same time that door opened and the lights brightened. Three people were standing in the doorway. They were all black and talking to each, but it was hard to understand what they were saying.

"Oh my God," said Phillip when the alarm went off. They had gone through many doors without trouble as they made their way to the nearest colony room, but when they opened that door, the alarm blared; they hadn't known, and neither had Archie, that after 10:30 PM an automatic alarm was armed on all the colony doors in case of some unlikely night-time escape when no one was present.

"Let's get out of here!" shouted Phillip.

"No! Wait," said Cindy. "We have to get at least some of them out."

They looked into the room and saw cells on both sides of the long concrete hallway. The odor was strong. "Come on," said Rudy.

They stepped into the room and looked into the first two cells. There was a young woman in one and a teenage boy with acne in the cell across from her. They seemed more like wild animals than humans.

"Let's at least get two of them," said Cindy. "You get him," she said, pushing Philip toward the boy's cell and handing him one of the pair of bolt cutters. "Get her," she said to Rudy.

Cindy opened one of the bags and pulled out two dark robes. Her father had said that getting any of them into clothes would be hard, but they couldn't step out of the building naked.

Everyone in the room was yelling. Two loud metallic pops announced that the locks on the cells had been snapped. Philip opened the door to the boy's cell, but didn't know what to do when the boy fled to the back and snarled at him, baring a partial set of ugly teeth; he seemed willing to fight.

Cindy pushed her husband out of the way and stepped into the concrete cell with the woman who was also huddled in the back of the cell. Cindy squatted down and took a deep breath.

"We have to go!" shouted Philip, and the young man in front of him yelled something loudly.

"Miriam!" yelled Levi. "Are you ok?"

Miriam looked at the black figure crouched in front of her.

Cindy pulled off her balaclava and gave the woman a smile. She said, "It's ok. We won't hurt you." She held out her hand and said, "Please. You should come with us."

"I'm ok," shouted Miriam over the din. "I think they want us to go with them."

"They're Germans!" yelled Levi, still baring his teeth and keeping the figure in front of him at bay. "They'll hurt us."

Miriam wasn't sure. The woman in front of her was more beautiful than anyone she had ever seen. She didn't have words for her hair; it was bright and smooth and the woman's eyes seemed caring, she was looking at her in a way that she had seen only in Miriam and Levi.

Miriam reached out and touched the woman's hand. "My name is Miriam. The man is Levi," she said, motioning to him.

"This is fucking nuts, we gotta go!" yelled Phillip as the alarm continued to blare. "If they won't come, leave them!"

Cindy's father had told her that they would be hard to understand, and that they might have a hard time communicating, but she was nearly certain that the woman had said that her name was Miriam and that the boy's name was Levi. She reached out and lightly touched Miriam's shoulder. "Miriam," she said. "Miriam," said Miriam. "Levi," she said, looking over her shoulder and then back at Miriam. "Levi," said Miriam.

Cindy stood up and held out her hand. Miriam took it and stood up.

"Throw me a robe," she said to Rudy.

It surprised Cindy that Miriam seemed to have made up her mind to trust her all at once. Although it was awkward, she let Cindy help her into the robe and tie the belt around her waste. Cindy pulled her mask back down and led Miriam out of the cell and over to Levi.

"Come with me Levi. I think they are from Outside. I think it's ok."

The Nelson's phone rang. Archie looked up at the clock above the television. It was a little after 2:30. He didn't expect the phone to wake his wife.

"Hello," he said, "This is Dr. Nelson."

"Heil Hitler. This is Orpo Hauptmann Helmut Arendt, head of security at Joseph Mengele. I'm sorry to disturb you Dr. Nelson, I do not believe we have met."

"No Hauptmann Arendt, I don't believe we have met. Is there a problem? I've been up watching the news about the fires. It's terrible."

"Yes Dr. Nelson, er, I mean no. Well, there is a problem at the hospital, but it has nothing to do with the fires. I called Dr. Eckel right away, but he said that I should first consult with you. There's been a break-in at the subhuman colony; two of the Jews were stolen."

"I'll be right there Hauptmann." Only two? He went upstairs to dress and try to wake his wife.

A couple of months after Dr. Kal's death, the Orpo had pulled back some of the guards it had placed at the homes of the extended families of the scientists who had received the death threats. Rudy and Cindy were still shadowed by SiPo agents, but the agents remained in the apartment building's lobby and no longer waited outside their door. Cindy and Rudy had learned that there were ways in and out the building that bypassed the lobby and their shadows. The agents didn't have any reason to imagine that their wards were trying to escape their protection.

The Third Part

Rudy drove out of town and pulled into the large parking lot of a Road-Ready truck stop just to the southeast of the city.

"There it is," said Phillip from the passenger seat and pointed to a white van with a carpet cleaning logo on its side.

They pulled up next to it, parking in the opposite direction. The side doors faced each other. Cindy was in the back with Miriam and Levi who sat huddled closely together. Talking had been very difficult, as she knew it would be, and the darkness had made it impossible to see their faces very well. But when the van stopped and turned off its engine, she could tell that they were both immediately on alert.

"Let's do this as quick as we can," said Phillip. He got out and opened the side door. A woman got out of the other van and slid their door open.

"We must be quick," she said.

Cindy took Miriam's hand and said in what she hoped was a reassuring tone, "Come. It's OK."

Miriam started to get out, but Levi held back and held on to her. "I'm afraid," he said. "What's going to happen to us?"

Cindy could make out only bits and pieces of what they were saying to each other but she could tell they were having a disagreement and that Miriam was consoling him and urging Levi to get out as well. Finally, he got out of the van with her.

Everyone stood between the two vans for a moment. Cindy motioned for them to get into the second vehicle. Finally, she got in herself, reached out and took Miriam's hand; Miriam followed her into the van pulling Levi along with her. She got them settled into the back seats and gave Miriam a hug. Miram seemed to understand that Cindy was saying good-bye. Cindy turned to get out of the van and Miriam shouted.

Cindy reassured her as well as she could, but finally pulled her hand away and gave her one final smile. She stepped out and the woman slid the door shut with a slam. She looked into Cindy's eyes, reached out and touched her shoulder and said, "God bless you honey."

"Let's go!" said Phillip as he jumped back into the van. Rudy started the engine as Cindy hopped in the back and pushed the door shut. She was shaking; tears were welling up.

Miriam and Levi huddled in the back as the van drove out of the parking lot. A man was driving. The woman moved to the back and sat down next to them on the bench seat.

"You must be frightened," she said, but neither of them could understand her. The woman saw the confusion in their faces.

Miriam said, "Miriam," and patted her chest. She reached over and put her hand on Levi's chest and said, "Levi."

The woman nodded. "Levi and Miriam. Nice to know you. I'm Marge. Marge Lutz."

Miriam and Levi looked confused, though in the dim light it was hard to tell. Marge patted her own chest and said slowly, "Marge."

"Marge," said Miriam. Marge smiled at her.

Marge opened a cooler and took out two sandwiches wrapped in cellophane. "You must be hungry." She handed one to each of them. Miriam took one, but Levi sat frozen, leaning hard against her.

Miriam looked at the thing in her hand. She held it to her nose and sniffed it. "What is it?" said Levi in a tone that signaled his distrust.

"I don't know. Smell it. It smells nice." She held it to Levi's nose.

"You're probably thirsty too," said Marge and pulled two cans of pop from the cooler and set them in a cup holder attached to the back of the front seats.

They didn't know what the sandwiches or the soft drink cans were, so they just left them sitting.

Marge felt the van accelerate and knew they had pulled onto the highway and were heading further southeast along the Illinois River. "It's a shame its so dark outside, the scenery is really nice along the river."

Although they couldn't understand what she was saying, somehow the woman's endless monologue made them feel a little more relaxed.

Archie was sitting at the far end of the table. At the opposite end was North American Oberstgruppenführer Heinz Schimmelpfennig. Closest to Schimmelpfennig were Orpo Hauptmann Helmut Arendt, acting head of security at Joseph Mengele, and Mengele Chief of Staff Otto Eckel.

Major Klaus Waldschmidt, acting commander of the RUC Orpo and a few uniformed Orpo officers and some others in street clothes who Archie took to be SiPo agents were at the table as well. All eyes were on the large video screen on the wall.

The surveillance videos from various cameras had been edited together. The scenes were time stamped with a yellow digital font. It began with a late model dark Ford van coming through the entrance of the parking ramp; the license plate had been obscured. The video cut to scenes from within the building. Scenes changed as the three darkly dressed invaders moved from room to room. The video image was poor and the dimmed lights added to the graininess of the picture. When they got to the colony room and the lights brightened, so did the image quality, but their faces were hidden. It seemed clear that there were two men and a woman, but Archie didn't know whether his perceptions were shared or not, and he didn't offer his opinion. The video showed that they had had difficulty getting the Jews out of their cells and into dark robes; the tape continued as the five backtracked the way they had come. It concluded with a shot of the van leaving the parking ramp.

The screen went blue. Oberstgruppenführer Schimmelpfennig inhaled and exhaled loudly; the displeasure in his sigh was palpable. "So! Hauptmann Arendt?"

"Without the license number it will be hard to identify the vehicle Oberstgruppenführe. We know only that it was a Ford, no more than five years old, and that it was dark. We don't even have a definite color. So far, we have identified 328 possibles in Chicago, 1,219 in the surrounding area, and 12,237 in the Midwest. But it could have been from anywhere. We are trying to narrow the list by screening for suspicious names."

"Dr. Nelson," said Schimmelpfennig, and all eyes turned toward him. Is there a public health risk? Were the subhumans infected with any dangerous germs?"

"I have thoroughly reviewed the subjects' medical records Oberstgruppenführer, and I can certify that they are medically clean. There is no public health risk."

"Well, thank God for that small miracle." He turned his attention back to Arendt, "And what of the pass card used? What have you discovered?"

"We have the employee in custody. His name is John F. Bowden. We are looking carefully into his ancestry. He swears that he lost his card a week or so ago but was afraid to report it. He doesn't know exactly when he lost it, he says."

"Do you believe him?"

"He's very frightened; it's hard to say. But the interrogation has really only just begun; we will know much more about him in a few days."

Schimmelpfennig closed his eyes. The situation had gone from bad, to worse, to unthinkable. He was answering hourly questions from Germany now. It had been impossible to keep the media silent; the fires on campus were too big and had blazed for too long. Two newspapers had received messages from radical covert groups claiming responsibility. One of the letters had mentioned the break-in at the hospital.

He opened his eyes and looked at the men around the table. He was filled with grave doubts about an immediate breakthrough and did not relish having to report the dismal news to Berlin. "Dismissed!" he barked, and even Dr. Eckel scurried away.

The sky was brightening when the van exited the highway and turned due west onto a two-lane blacktop. Levi had relaxed a little. He and Miriam stared out at the alien landscape as the sun began to set ablaze endless fields of foot-high corn. The window was down about an inch. Strange but somehow familiar scents washed over them. A light wind was blowing just hard enough to send ripples across the sea of corn shoots. They had absolutely no idea how to make sense of the flashing green and gold undulations and the infinite and quickly brightening sky above it all.

Marge was watching them. "It's beautiful, isn't it?"

The corn sea ran for miles, and they traveled through it for just over an hour when the van began to slow. "Keep 'em down," said the driver.

Marge touched Miriam on the arm and got her and Levi's attention. She knelt down on the floorboard and motioned them down next to her. Miriam understood immediately and said something to Levi. The van came to a stop and after a few long moments drove on again. A few minutes later the driver said, "Ok," and Marge sat back up. Miriam and Levi followed her lead.

The driver looked into his rearview mirror and finally made eye conduct. Levi was looking at him. He said, "Another hour, and we'll be there. That was the only damned stop light in the county. Y'all'll be safe out here."

"They don't understand a thing you're sayin' Frank," laughed Marge.

But Levi did get part of the man's message. He wasn't sure what he had said, but the man's face was open and caring. These definitely weren't Germans.

Rudy and Cindy had slipped easily and without notice back into their apartment. They were in bed and snuggled closely together and whispering into each other's ear.

"I hope they're ok," said Cindy.

"You were amazing," whispered Rudy. "No matter what happens, they are better off than they were. Man, the smell, and all the yelling. Some of them looked really horrible. I thought Phillip was going to pee his pants."

Cindy laughed quietly and said, "I know, but he did ok, considering the danger. I was scared every second."

"I hope the fires weren't too bad. I think they must have saved us when the alarm went off. I thought I was going to pee my pants."

"I'm sleeping in tomorrow," said Cindy, and she turned over spooning into Rudy's lap.

Rudy put his arm around her and pulled her closer. "Me too, but since we're up now…". He rose up on his elbow and pulled her onto her back. He kissed her gently. "I love you."

The van slowed and turned onto a gravel road; the tires crunched. After a few minutes, it pulled up and parked next to an old well-maintained white clapboard farmhouse. "We're home," said Marge. "You're going to like it here."

Marge slid open the door, and stepped out into the yard. "I gotta let Lady out." She walked away and headed to the house. Miriam and Levi huddled together looking out the door and the windows. After years of almost no sensory stimulation, they were struggling to make sense of the kaleidoscope before them.

Frank came around to the door and sat down on floorboard, his feet on the ground. He heard a screen door bang shut and smiled over at Miriam and Levi, "Here comes Lady."

A brown and black longhaired dog of questionable pedigree ran up to the van and put her front paws in Frank's lap. Her tail was wagging energetically as she licked his face. Frank was bubbling over her.

Miriam and Levi watched the scene with mixed emotion. Lady noticed them and jumped into the van to investigate, but Frank said something and she jumped back down. Frank looked at Miriam and patted the floorboard next to him. She understood what he wanted and said to Levi, "I think we should do what they say. They seem nice."

"I'm scared. What is that?"

"I think it's a dog. Miriam told me about them, remember? I told you that she said they lick you and make you smile. The man seems to like it. I'm going to sit out here."

Miriam got up and sat down next to Frank. Lady immediately began sniffing her. Miriam was tense, but Frank seemed relaxed, so she tried to be calm. Frank took her hand and held it gently while lady smelled her; he put her hand on Lady's head and showed her how to pet her. Miriam was mesmerized by her silkiness and warmth, she was reminded somehow of her baby, Nick.

Marge reappeared and said, "Let's get them into the house."

"All right," said Frank. "I think Miriam will go with me, but I'm not sure about Levi."

"He seems pretty dependent on her right now; I'll bet he'll come with her."

"Ok." Frank stood up and offered Miriam his hand again.

"They want us to go somewhere. Come on," she said to Levi.

Levi reluctantly left what he took to be the safety of the van and stepped outside. Lady immediately turned her attention to him. Levi stood frozen as she sniffed him all over.

"It's ok," said Marge for the hundredth time and took Levi's hand.

Frank and Miriam led the way and Marge and Levi followed. Birds chirped from the wires overhead and crowded around a feeder on a pole in the yard. Swallows were wheeling overhead. Chickens were scratching in the dust and pecking here and there in the grass. A rooster crowed. Cows were lowing somewhere nearby. The sun was gleaming down brightly. They walked slowly to the house; Frank and Marge felt as though they were leading victims of a recent disaster who were still in shock, or maybe babies just learning to walk and seeing the world for the first time.

Trish put another slice of apple pie on Rudy's plate and handed it to Mary, who passed it down.

"I have to stop taking this second slice," he said, "I'm going to get fat."

"You're skin and bones," she laughed. "Cindy, you're not cooking enough for Rudy."

"Who has time to cook, Mom? With classes getting ready to start up, all we've been doing is scheduling and buying books. Did we tell you that

Rudy's going to be a TA in Jackson's Intro to Political Science this term?"

"That's great," said Archie. "How's the construction going on campus?"

"They say that the library will definitely be open," said Rudy, "I've heard that they may not rebuild the steam plant, apparently the other two are more modern and can do the job. Kaiser Union is still being worked on; but I can't imagine that they won't have something open on campus somewhere to get lunch and a beer."

"Let's just hope there isn't another attack this year," said Trish. "I'm sick of all that."

Cindy smiled at her father and said, "Who's your teacher going to be this year Mary?"

One of the first things they taught them, even before they were able to converse, was how to hide. Frank had remodeled a bedroom as soon as they'd heard that a couple of people might need a place to hide. One of his ancestors had run a boarding house down in Kansas that was a layover on the Underground Railroad; there was never a moment or even a sliver of doubt in his mind or in his heart that providing refuge from the predations of society and government was an absolute duty of an ethical man. Marge wasn't quite so dramatic; she simply said "Of course," when she heard that people might need a place to hide.

Frank moved a wall and hid the door to the cellar behind a false back wall of a new closet. The basement had an entrance from the outside as well; he built a new wall in the basement out of old materials that matched the basement well; only a very careful inspection would reveal the hidden space behind it.

The small secret basement room had narrow bunk beds, a small desk area, and a dry toilet. A small closet was lined with shelves holding jugs of water and a variety of ready-to-eat foods.

But teaching Miriam and Levi how to hide quickly was the easiest of the very many things that they needed to learn. Even eating and drinking had turned out to need practice.

When they brought Miriam and Levi into the house for the first time, the Lutz's were confronted with two new guests who knew absolutely nothing about the world. Nudity meant nothing to them, which Marge and Frank had learned quickly when they dropped their robes on the floor. Marge had led them around the house by hand. Every little thing was a discovery, a mystery, and sometimes a cause for fear. In the kitchen, Marge had shown them the sink.

Tell Me Your Story

When she turned on the tap, Levi cowered and moved against the far fall. "They're going to spray us!" he cried. But Miriam had already willingly put her full trust into these two strangers' hands.

"Levi!" she snapped. "These people aren't Germans. I don't understand anything that's going on. Why did those other people take us out of the lab? I don't know, but I could tell that they were afraid too. Levi! These people are trying to help us. We should trust them."

Levi seemed to shake himself. He stretched his head this way and that and finally looked squarely at Marge and then over to Miriam.

"Ok. You're right. They aren't Germans. I won't be afraid any more. I'll try." He looked back at Marge, walked up to her and looked into her eyes. "Levi," he said, patting his chest. He reached out and touched Marge lightly. "Marge." Then he stepped around her and put his mouth to the tap.

"Come taste this!" he shouted to Miriam. Lady jumped up and put her paws on the counter to see what all the excitement was about.

Marge watched them slake their thirst. When they backed away from the faucet, she showed them how to turn it on and off. Just that little lesson consumed half an hour. Then she showed them the cupboard that held the glasses and took three of them out. She filled her glass and then took a sip. "Go on," she said. "It's easier than putting your mouth around the faucet." Miriam snorted a nose full the first time she tried to drink, but Marge didn't laugh and Levi was obviously concerned; Marge was appalled by what this said about their lives in the labs. She understood why they hadn't seemed to be interested in the sandwiches or the sodas she had offered them in the van.

The first days were the hardest. Hygiene was an ordeal. The shower frightened both of them. Frank and Marge took turns standing in the shower and washing in front of them to help them over their fear. They assumed that something had happened to them that made spraying water an unpleasant thing. Miriam went first. She stepped into the shower with Marge and held her arms tight to her body. She let Marge wash her; waves of grime and filth were washed down the drain.

With Frank and Marge coaxing and Miriam scolding they were eventually able to bathe Levi as well. Then came the clippers.

They both had years of matted, unwashed hair hanging in dreadlocks. Marge had wanted to try brushing out Miriam's, but Miriam didn't like the pulling, so Marge gave up and turned them both over to Frank.

The noise of the clippers was a new ordeal; it reminded them of some of the tools the German's used on them. But they didn't struggle too much. Frank cut all their hair off. Afterwards, they rubbed and rubbed their bald heads, and then took turns rubbing each other's.

Clothes and dressing were particularly hard. Everything seemed to make them itch.

Furniture was an oddity to them. They quickly understood though that sitting on a couch or lying on a bed was more comfortable than the floor. Everything was a revelation.

One day, Marge took a large children's picture book from one of the many bookcases in the house and sat down on the worn green velvet couch with Miriam and Levi on each side of her. "I know you can't understand a lot of what I'm saying right now, but you will. Today, you are going to start learning how to read." She opened the book and pointed to the first picture. "Dog," she said. Miriam and Levi each said "dog," back to her. She pointed to the word below the picture. "Dog." Lady was sitting with her head on Levi's knee.

Classes at the Reich had begun without incident. Der Prüfer, the student newspaper, dedicated its first edition to the fires that had ravaged the campus and the construction underway to repair the damage. No mention was made of the bombs or the Jews taken from Mengele.

Shortly after the first quarter's marks were posted, another brochure appeared on campus. This one, "Behind the Laboratory Door," was widely distributed. It had grainy photos and explained in graphic detail what was happening in one of the labs. Excerpts started showing up in the licensed "alternative" paper on campus, Der Ikonoklast. And even though video cameras were everywhere on campus, all they recorded were people with obscured faces leaving stacks of brochures in the library, in the union, and here and there around campus. Professors were increasingly being asked about the use of Jews and other subhumans in the Reich's labs and in the labs across town at Joseph Mengele Memorial Hospital for Genetic and Racial Disease. Der Prüfer was receiving letters daily about the fires, the bombs, and the Jews at Mengele.

University president Hans-Dieter Wendt was fuming. He paced back and forth and heaped buckets of scorn on Major Waldschmidt. "Herr Major, I will not have another year like the last one; what have you been doing over the summer? Have you accomplished nothing?"

"Herr Wendt, you must know that the Order Police has committed its massive resources to the investigation and to the school's security. I know that Berlin has been monitoring the situation very intently. The North American Oberstgruppenführer is in constant contact with them."

"But have you arrested anyone?" Wendt shouted.

"We have Herr Wendt, but, alas, like that student last year, the few people we've arrested have all simply picked up literature from a large pile that they have found somewhere, and have spread it around. They know nothing, I can assure you of that; our interrogation methods have been rigorous and professional. I recommend making the distribution of anti-Reich literature a cause for immediate expulsion."

"And what do we do about the scientific papers themselves Major Wendt?"

"I'm not sure I follow you Herr Wendt."

"That shows me the Orpo aren't doing their fucking job God-damn it! Now the students are passing around scientific journal articles. And look at this!"

Wendt opened a manila folder and took out a few pages stapled together and pushed them toward Waldschmidt. The Orpo Major picked them up expecting to see the title of some scientific paper, but it was an application to start a new student club on campus. The required five students had signed their names and a faculty member, a professor of comparative literature, had signed as an advisor. They wanted to call their new club, "Students Against Subhuman Experiments".

"Should we expel them, Herr Major?"

"Maybe you should help them, Herr Wendt."

Rebbe Shrinkle had been receiving occasional updates about the two people liberated from the lab. He had learned that they were speaking better and that it was time to get them each a set of identification papers. A set of photos had been slowly moved from Illinois to New York, and he had passed them on to a Jewish document forger he knew well.

He had also heard that they were both in need of medical care. The man needed some kind of dental work and the woman had some sort of chronic pain in her leg. And, they might both need glasses. He wasn't sure how to arrange for so much medical help so far away, but he was loath to tell them to proceed on their own because of the extreme risk and the high importance of keeping them safe.

The weather had turned cold. Students hurried from building to building bundled against the arctic blast scouring the campus. Cindy stepped into Henry Ford Hall and headed for the second floor where her accounting class was held. She stopped short at the bulletin board next to the stairs. An oversized poster announced that a debate was going to be held between the president of a new student club, "Students Against Subhuman Experiments," and Dr. Ermingard Gottlieb, a professor of humanities and genetics, it was titled: "Subhuman Research: Pro and Con."

Cindy read over the poster a few times; she'd never heard of this club and wondered why the university had sanctioned it, let alone was providing a venue for a debate. She jotted down the information about time and place and hurried on to her class.

That night she and Rudy were lying together in bed. "Do you want to go?" he whispered into her ear.

Cindy turned over. "Do you?" she whispered back.

Rudy got out of bed and said aloud, "Let's see what the weather holds." He clicked on the radio and got back into bed.

"I guess," he whispered. "It seems like your father's threat letter might make you interested in the subject, not to mention the SiPos who have been following us around. Would it look odd if we didn't go?"

"It won't look odd either way; let's go."

In just a few months, Levi and Miriam were able to converse with Marge and Frank with some ease. Miriam and Levi continued to talk between themselves in a dialect that was only partially understandable to the Lutzes.

Levi was sprawled on the floor on an old, somewhat thread-worn maroon oriental carpet. Lady walked over to him, flopped down and rolled over on her back. She looked at him with a big grin. Levi sat up and began rubbing her chest and stomach. Frank glanced over at Marge and they gave each other a little smile.

Miriam was crouching on her feet in a large chair. She had an encyclopedia open to an article on geography that was filled with colorful pictures of people in other countries wearing traditional clothes.

"Have you been to Jah-pan?" she said.

"Japan," said Marge. "No, we haven't been there honey."

Miriam opened a small notebook and carefully copied the word Japan.

61

She had been keeping her list for almost a month. The printing was becoming more legible and uniform, and she was just beginning to make a few brief notes next to some of the words she added to her growing list.

"You spoil that dog, Levi," said Frank. "Before you got here she was lucky to get her belly scratched two or three times a week."

"Lady," said Levi. "She nice. What we make for dinner?"

Once Levi broke through his reluctance to try out new foods, food had become his favorite thing. Marge had been having him help her in the kitchen. He had already begun doing some cooking under her watchful eye.

"How does spaghetti sound?" she said.

"With that bread?" he asked.

"French bread. Sure. Do you remember how to make the dough?"

"Maybe." He headed into the kitchen with Lady at his heals.

"I guess it's time to start dinner," Marge laughed, and followed him in.

Frank watched Miriam. Her arms and hands were severely scarred. He and Marge had been reluctant to ask too many questions about the labs. Miriam turned a page and looked up at him.

"Something?" she asked.

Frank leaned forward in his chair; he put his hand on his forearm and rubbed it. He looked at Miriam's arms and nodded his head a little, "What happened to your arms?"

Miriam looked at him for a moment. "Eat them."

Frank looked confused. Miriam put her arm in her mouth and feigned biting them. "Eat them."

"Why?"

"Later," she answered. "My words are not good enough now. I will tell you. You will tell me your story."

"Of course," said Frank, but he didn't think she had asked him a question, it sounded more like a statement. These two were odd in many ways, he thought to himself.

After dinner, they all sat in front of the television and watched a sitcom about a retired couple in Alaska who were running a summer Nazi Youth camp. Levi and Miriam repeated out loud some of the words and phrases they heard. Marge figured that it was all part of the crash course on appearing normal.

University president Hans-Dieter Wendt had to admit that Orpo Major

Waldschmidt was right. It was the smart thing to do. Help the group establish itself. It would be a magnet for the radicals. He had begun to think that "Students Against Subhuman Experiments" could be just the ticket for finding out who was sympathetic to this pathetic and disloyal radicalism.

Wendt's office had suggested the debate, and the students had accepted. Orpo would be able to photograph and identify everyone who attended. It was a perfect piece of bait.

He had spent some time considering who the best representative would be, the best person to stand up and crush the stupid idea that subhumans were not the perfect research subjects for Reich scientists to use. He had toyed with asking that doctor over at Mengele, Dr. Nelson his name was, since he wasn't Race and had good knowledge of how the Jews and the other subjects were cared for. But he worried that he might not be a convincing speaker.

Dr. Ermingard Gottlieb was the perfect choice. She was well liked by her students. She spoke on the national circuit about the anthropology and genetics of the races. Her husband, Dr. Paul Gottlieb, was a medical doctor who had trained in Austria. They were both Race, brilliant, and attractive.

The Richard Wagner Auditorium was only a third full. Two lecterns stood a few meters from each other in the center of the stage. To the left was a small table and chair. The lights dimmed and Wendt walked on to the stage and over to the small table. He picked up the microphone.

"Welcome. I'm glad that you came tonight, though the turnout is a little disappointing. Maybe the low turnout says something about the relative unimportance of this matter to most of our students and staff."

"A lot of people were probably afraid to come," whispered Rudy into Cindy's ear.

"As you all know, our beloved university was attacked by terrorists at the beginning of last summer's break," continued Wendt.

"Reich University has never shied away from examining controversial issues. Here at Reich, we pride ourselves on our continual and fearless sifting and winnowing of the facts by which alone truth can be found. With this great idea in mind, we decided that we would set an example for those who criticize and disagree with our honorable work by organizing this debate over the use of subhumans in scientific research.

"Taking the affirmative side of the argument will be our illustrious colleague, Dr. Ermingard Gottlieb."

Gottlieb walked on to the stage. She was a tall imposing woman. Her long dark hair was streaked with gray and arranged neatly in a coiled braid pinned to the back of her head. She wore a black on black formal pantsuit of flowing silk. A striking gold Swastika medallion hung from a fine chain around her neck. She stopped at center stage.

"Dr. Gottlieb is known internationally for her groundbreaking work on the genetics of race, the eugenics of race purity, and the history of science.

"The contrary position will be argued by Wilhelm Schott."

Schott entered the stage from the opposite side. He was a handsome young man. His blond hair was a little unkempt, but his dark blazer and light trousers were neat. He was sporting a small goatee. He stopped at center stage next to his opponent and looked over at Wendt.

"Mr. Schott is a junior humanities major and the president of the student club, 'Students Against Subhuman Experiments.'

"Please join me in giving them a warm Reich welcome."

The small audience responded with polite applause. "You may each take your places behind a podium." They shook hands and took their places.

"Our format tonight will be as follows: Questions were submitted by each of our participants. I will read alternating questions. First, one posed by Mr. Schott, and then one posed by Dr. Gottlieb, and so on. The respondent will have three minutes to answer, and the poser will have two minutes for follow-up; the respondent will then have one minute for a final follow-up.

"We will continue in this manner for one hour at which time we will entertain questions submitted by the audience. Ushers will be walking the aisles with note cards and pencils for you to write down your questions. They will bring me the note cards, and I will select the questions to ask. The question and answer session is scheduled for thirty minutes, but if interest warrants, we might extend the time. Dr. Gottlieb and Mr. Schott have both agreed ahead of time to this format. Let us begin.

"The first question is for you Dr. Gottlieb: 'Jews, the negroid races, and the other subhumans being used in research suffer like we would if we were being used. Shouldn't we follow the Golden Rule?"

"Thank you for that thoughtful question Willy. Do you mind if I call you Willy? And thank you Dr. Wendt for putting together this forum," she said without pausing to hear Schott's response. "And thank you to the audience, especially you students who took part of your precious free time to come and learn even more than is required of you by your instructors.

"Would you repeat the question please Dr.Wendt, I do hope that my thank-yous won't be deducted from my time."

"Of course not Dr. Gottlieb. I'll repeat the question: 'Jews, the negroid races, and the other subhumans being used in research suffer like we would if we were being used. Shouldn't we follow the Golden Rule? Your time begins now."

"So, I think this is really two questions. Do I get extra time?" Gottlieb smiled at Wendt.

"Let me answer the easy question first: 'Should we follow the Golden Rule?' Of course we should; we should treat each other with respect, as we are doing here in this debate. Was it the Golden Rule that led to the terrorists trying to burn down our great university? But whether we should follow the Golden Rule is a moral matter; science is concerned with facts, verifiable, testable, propositions.

"Your second question, Willy, actually a false premise that, I think, is at the root of all the misapprehension by your group, is whether or not subhumans feel things like we do; do they suffer like we imagine we would? Scientifically, we haven't been able to answer this question definitively. The precautionary principle demands us to remain skeptical until evidence proving us wrong becomes available. Right now the preponderance of evidence suggests that subhumans don't feel things like Caucasians do.

"I hope the rest of the questions are this easy to answer," she said. A few quiet chuckles could be heard from the audience.

"Mr. Schott. Your response?"

"Well, thank you Dr. Wendt for organizing this important event, and thank you Dr. Gottlieb for agreeing to participate. And thank you to everyone in the audience."

Schott looked down at his notes. "But, Dr. Gottlieb, experiments that have gone on right here in Chicago have been based on the fact that Aryan and subhuman nervous systems are so similar that discoveries made, say, by experimenting on a Jew's brain can be applied directly to Aryans. If our nervous systems are so similar, doesn't it mean that we are feeling the same things?"

Gottlieb answered without waiting for Wendt's invitation. "Similar does not mean identical. Very strict regulations are in place to assure that discoveries made using subhumans are tested in Aryans in tightly controlled experiments prior to wide-scale marketing or utilization. I think you need to do your homework, Willy."

Wendt smiled to himself. He had made a good choice with Gottlieb. "The next question is for you Mr. Schott: 'Should we test new drugs and chemicals directly on Aryans and skip subhuman testing? What about pediatric drugs? Should we test them on Race babies?'"

"No one is saying that drugs should be tested only on Aryans. We're saying that they shouldn't be tested on subhumans either. There are lots of alternatives. We could use lower animals; we could use human tissue cultures, computer models, imaging technology, and other more humane methods. It's cruel to use subhumans. There is good evidence that they are just like us Dr. Gottlieb. Look at the cultures they produced before the war. Look at the books they've written, the music and the art they've produced. You can't deny the plain facts.

"I've read that all new drugs are risky. I've read that until thousands and thousands of people have taken them that we don't have a good idea of their long-term consequences. So, at some point, a baby will be given a drug that no other baby has ever been given. Don't we actually test new drugs on Aryan babies in just this way?

"Dr. Gottlieb? Two minutes," prompted Wendt.

"First, I am offended Wilhelm by your use of the term cruel. You make it sound like the people using subhumans enjoy what that they are doing. I can assure you and the audience that their work isn't at all cruel. It is highly regulated. The subjects always get the best of care, just like in a regular hospital. It they weren't well cared for, the results might be skewed. Good scientists like those here at Reich and across town at Mengele, demand healthy subjects for their research.

"Second, lower animals can be good for studying the most basic biological phenomena, but when it comes to studying the metabolism and functioning of an Aryan, the only good model, not a perfect model as I said earlier, the only good model, the tool we are ethically required to use for the good of the Race, is the subhuman.

"And third, all this about their cultures, their art, and on and on, well, I've studied these questions very carefully. I'm a racial anthropologist and I have traveled the world studying these so-called cultures of the subhuman races. I can say categorically that in every single case we've studied to date, all we have found is poor imitation of existing Aryan invention and idea; and usually very poor imitation at that. We have yet to discover even one original or unique idea or invention or much of anything directly attributable to a subhuman culture; in fact, we don't use the word culture any longer when writing or speaking about subhumans. Racial anthropologists now use the term, group."

"You say they are well cared for Dr. Gottlieb, but undercover photos and leaked documents say differently," responded Schott.

"The next question…," started Wendt, but he was interrupted by Dr. Gottlieb.

"I'm sorry. I know I don't get to respond, but let's put this matter of the brochures and the so-called undercover photos to rest right now. Those photos were not from here. They were grainy and appeared to be doctored. You can do anything with a computer these days."

"Dr. Wendt, I demand a chance to respond," Schott said into the microphone.

"Please, Dr. Gottlieb," cautioned Wendt. "Everyone is as emotional about this as you are. But let's keep to the format, please. How would it look for the Reich president to lose control? I tell all my staff to maintain strict classroom control."

A few laughs from the audience softened the tense moment.

"Thirty seconds, to be fair. Mr. Schott?" said Wendt.

"Those pictures look real to me and to other students I've talked to. If they aren't real, give us a tour of the labs Dr. Wendt."

"That's an interesting idea Mr. Schott, but one I will have to consider at a later date. Let's move on to the next question.

"This one is for you Dr. Gottlieb, and it goes to Mr. Schott's last comment: Until the brochures were published last year most students did not even know that these kinds of things were happening here. If the subhumans are well-cared for and treated humanely, why is it so secret?"

"There is absolutely nothing secret about it," said Gottlieb. "The scientists here publish hundreds of papers in scientific journals every year talking about their research. Openness is a hallmark of science. Why didn't the students know about the research? Who can say? But the library is filled with these journals. If the students didn't know about the important research here at Reich, then we need to do a better job at calling their attention to it. This university is at the forefront of world-class science and all of us should be proud to be affiliated with Reich.

"I also know that entry into the labs and the subhuman colonies is highly controlled, for the health of the subhumans. Special vaccinations are required —vaccinations developed using subhumans, I might add— before anyone is allowed in. I'm not an expert on this; maybe during the Q and A someone from one of the labs can clarify this for us.

"I dare say that all this talk about secret cruel labs is distressing and a complete affront to the high ethics and goals of the scientists here."

"Mr. Schott?"

"Thank you Dr. Wendt. But it is secret Dr. Gottlieb. We have tried to talk with students who have worked in the labs and they say that they've been ordered not to talk about anything that goes on in them. The journals you mentioned give only a few details of the experiments, though even those few details can be hair-raising, and they almost never say where the experiments took place.

"Dr. Gottlieb, I am a Political Science major. I don't keep up with geology, or breakthroughs in chemistry, or medicine. Do you keep up with every field? Moreover, geology, chemistry, math, these other fields aren't loaded with the ethical problems that subhuman experimentation is. Why isn't the university encouraging debate about this?"

"Quickly, Dr. Gottlieb," said Wendt.

"Much of what goes on in the labs is proprietary, Willy. If competitors could find out what a lab is doing they might steal an idea. The university is encouraging debate; I mean, here we are after all."

Rudy leaned over to Cindy again," I thought she said that openness was a hallmark of science?"

The questions continued back and forth until Dr. Wendt announced that the time had expired and that he would begin asking questions from the audience. He said, "I have been sorting through the audience's questions and will read some of them one at a time. Dr Gottlieb and Mr. Schott will each be given two minutes to respond, with a follow-up at my discretion.

"Here's the first question; I think it is directed at you Mr. Schott: Even if what you say is true about subhumans being tortured in the labs, does this give anyone the right to use violence?"

"Thank you for that question. Students Against Subhuman Experiments is against all forms of violence. But it should be noted that no one was hurt in the fires last summer and hundreds of subhumans might be suffering and dying right now in the labs around campus. That's the real violence."

"Dr. Gottlieb."

"I don't know what to say. I'm stunned. Not real violence? How many police officers and firemen put their lives on the line to fight those fires? And let us not forget for one moment the razor blades sent in the mail. And can you really have no concern at all for Dr. Kals or his family. He had two young daughters. They won't get to know their father now."

Murmurs from the audience grew in volume.

"Quiet, please!" said Wendt. "The next question is for you Dr. Gottlieb: Please explain the oversight system and how humane care is guaranteed."

"Of course, and thank you for that question. All universities and laboratories are required to have a plan in place that spells out how the subhumans will be treated and cared for. This plan must be reviewed and approved by the World Reich Council on Humane Research. Every university and laboratory must have an Institutional Subhuman Care and Use Committee, an ISHCUC, that verifies and certifies that the experiments comply with the plan. I assure you that every facet of subhuman use is carefully regulated and monitored by caring and diligent scientists and regulators. The labs risk losing their certifications and licenses to use subhumans if they aren't in full compliance. And, I might add, each World Reich Council on Humane Research Zustände office conducts unannounced annual inspections of all the labs. You can be assured that the experts know what they are doing."

"Mr. Schott?"

"We have heard about these inspections, but we have been told that the inspection reports are not public information. As long as there is so much secrecy, university spokespersons can say whatever suits their needs and no one can challenge them with the facts.

"As I have been saying, from the little we have been able to find out, the conditions in the labs are miserable and many people are being tortured around the clock."

Someone in the audience shouted, "They aren't people!"

"Please be respectful," ordered Wendt. "Dr. Gottlieb, would you care to comment?"

"Well, in spite of their outburst, the comment was right. Subhumans aren't people, as we usually use the term. I don't have time here to explain the clear unambiguous genetic differences between Aryans and subhumans; I'll just assure the audience that these differences are real and probably account for our advanced intellect and sensitivities.

"The accusation of torture is too ludicrous and rude to comment on."

Orpo Major Waldschmidt was keeping his fingers crossed. The debate had been worthless as far new leads were concerned, everyone photographed was well known to Orpo and SiPo. Their motivations for attending were easily accounted for and understandable. The good news was that the university spokesperson had done such a good job. Since then, no new pamphlets had appeared and no one had received another threat. It was as if the students had tired of the issue. "Students Against Subhuman Experiments" was watched carefully, but their meetings were poorly attended. The students involved seemed to be dilettantes and only fashionably discontented with the university administration.

Major Waldschmidt had high hopes that the school year would end on a peaceful note and that he would be promoted.

Miriam and Levi had made good progress over the winter on their ability to speak clearly and to understand what was being said.

Tell Me Your Story

When Miriam and Levi had arrived at the beginning of summer, they had remained mostly in the house with easy access to their secret room in case someone showed up unexpectedly. This had happened only once, and they had disappeared quickly without notice. The Lutzes had entertained their visitor on the front porch.

It was late winter when their papers had finally arrived. They memorized the fabricated details of their heritage and family history. They worked to become fluent and offhand about made-up brothers and sisters and the small far-flung farm towns they could now talk about growing up in.

As winter grudgingly gave way to spring, they began spending more time out doors.

The Lutzes grew corn and had a small dairy. Miriam and Levi had been to the milking parlor only once before during an early tour of the farm. Then, everything was still surreal and hard to put into perspective. But now, Miriam was more relaxed and was beginning to make some sense of the world she was reading about and learning about on the television.

Frank finished pulling off the milking machines and opened the barn door. The eighteen cows he had just milked walked out into a fenced barnyard beginning to turn seriously muddy.

"Let's check the preggers," he said to Miriam and walked around the side of the barn. In the still barren field, ten black and white cows stood chewing their cud and ready to give birth.

"It won't be long now," he smiled at Miriam.

"I don't understand," she said.

"Oh. These cows are all going to have a calf soon, a baby cow. I inseminated all of them on the same day, just after you and Levi got here."

"What's in-sem-in-ate-ed?" she asked, writing the word in her notebook.

She listened carefully to Frank's explanation and to the hows and whys of dairy cow husbandry. Miriam looked at the ten cows standing in the mud. She thought back to the women's room in the colony. She wondered if they would love their babies like she had loved hers.

Rebbe Shrinkle was worried. The report had a sense of urgency and danger. According to the brief report, the woman had become violent and was demanding to leave the farm.

The Rebbe was unsure how to proceed. They couldn't simply let them walk away without being sure that they wouldn't disclose anything if they were caught, and he thought that they would be caught right away since they knew so little and might stick out and draw attention to themselves.

The trees were budding out again; a few early pink blossoms were showing on the apple trees. Early dandelions had been coaxed open by the warm sun and added their beauty to the already bright green hillside. Rudy was lying comfortably with his head in Cindy's lap. The wine bottle was nearly empty; the end of a loaf of French bread and a small piece of Gouda lay on plate next to them. Rudy picked up the cheese and nibbled a last bite and put the last small bit into Cindy's mouth. He swallowed and said, "What a year."

"I think Daddy's trying to come up with a way to get away from Mengele. He's hoping that he can get transferred or something. He told me he might even just quit."

"Your mom will love that."

"She still doesn't have a clue; she pretends that he's happy and that everything is ok. If he quits what do you think they'll do to us, or to me? Will they let me finish school?"

"I don't know. I think the longer he stays, the longer we're married, the less repercussions there will be. Burnout can't be too unusual or unexpected with that job.

"Hey, I can't believe I almost forgot to tell you, Phillip called and asked me if I want to help him study for his political science final."

"Does he need your help? I thought he was a good student."

"He is. He doesn't. I'm sure he wants to talk about something."

"Yeesh," said Cindy.

The cows began showing signs of labor about a day later. Miriam and Levi were on hand for each delivery. Lady seemed as fascinated at they were. The deliveries went smoothly, the mothers licked their babies clean, and each calf had finally stood on wobbly legs and started to suckle. Frank had counted himself lucky because the year before two of his cows had required a visit from the vet because of birthing complications.

After the deliveries, Frank had pulled ten calf hutches from behind the barn and set them up in a line about eight feet from each other. Then he got out the wire fencing and fenced a tiny yard in front of each of the white plastic little sheds. He spread straw in each one. Levi helped. As they worked, Frank explained to him what they were doing.

"In three days we'll put the calves in the hutches, so they can't suckle any more. If they could, they'd take all the milk and we wouldn't have any to sell."

The day came to separate the calves. One by one, Frank herded a cow and a calf into a chute and then forced the mother out into a corral while the calf was left behind. He then carried the calf to a hutch on the opposite side of the barn. The cow and the calf were mooing and crying.

"When are they going back with their mothers?" asked Miriam. "They are crying."

"They'll all be crying and bellowing for a couple days, until they get used to it," said Frank. "They'll settle down in a few days."

"But they want their babies," said Miriam.

"But the milk is how we make our living Miriam. We can't get milk without calves."

"Why do you let them stay with their mothers at all?" Miriam was remembering how much more she had cared about Nick than she had about Little Jen.

"Colostrum. The cows make mostly colostrum for the first three days. The calves have to have it. After that, we can feed them milk replacer from a bottle. You'll like that."

"Let's get another one Levi," Frank said, and headed off to round up another cow and calf.

Miriam shouted something to Levi in colony dialect that Frank couldn't understand. They exchanged a few words.

Miriam said, "I thought you raised corn?" Frank was nonplussed.

"We do raise corn. You know that. What's going on, what's wrong?"

"We never had milk in the labs. Why do you need milk? Why can't we eat corn? Can you sell corn?"

"Well Miriam, I still don't know what's going on here. We sell corn. Most of the corn we grow isn't that good to eat; it's ground up and used in lots of things. We grow some corn for corn-on-the-cob, but we don't grow enough to sell." Cows were bawling to their calves who were crying back at them. All the cows seemed to be on edge. Lady stood and watched sensing some sort of conflict.

"Come on Levi, we have to get the rest of them in the hutches before it gets dark."

"No," said Miriam.

Levi stood still watching Frank. Frank looked over at him and noticed how he had begun filling out. He wasn't the same thin pale frightened young man who had arrived on the farm almost a year before. "Levi?"

"The calves should be with their mothers," he said.

"What? This is about the cows? You're making too much of this," Frank said to Miriam. "People have been raising cows like this for years. Every farmer does it."

"Do you remember my story?"

"What? Oh. They took your babies. Miriam, you know how sorry we are about everything that was done to you. That's why we're hiding you here and trying to help you and Levi. But these are cows. They're just animals. This is the way things are supposed to be; this is the way things are. God gave us the animals."

Miriam stood quietly for a long minute. "We're just Jews."

SiPo had pulled most of its agents. A few scientists were still being watched over but Rudy and Cindy's shadows had been reassigned. In spite of the seeming reduced surveillance, Rudy and Phillip were still mindful of the microphones hidden around the campus.

Phillip picked up the pen he had dropped on the floor to get a look at the underside of the library table he and Rudy were sitting at.

"It's the two Jews. I guess the woman went kind of crazy. They've been on a farm, but they can't stay there any longer."

"What are we supposed to do about it?"

"As I understand it, the only people who have seen them are us and the two people who were driving the other van. I think they've been living with them. Someone has to take them some place new."

"Where?"

"I don't know yet. They want to keep the number of people who know about them as small as possible, so they want us to move them."

Rudy wondered again just who 'they' were, but didn't want to ask.

"Jeez. I'll have to talk to Cindy."

"I can't go," said Phillip.

"What do you mean? You have to go."

"I can't. I'm sorry. I just can't. I almost cracked the last time. You know that. I can't take the pressure. I'll let you know more when I hear." He stood up quickly and left.

The Fourth Part

Major Klaus Waldschmidt, acting commander of the RUC Orpo, picked up the phone in his office. "Heil Hitler, Oberstgruppenführer."

"Sieg Heil, Major. We may have a lead in the stolen Jew case," said North American Oberstgruppenführer Heinz Schimmelpfennig. "Orpo picked up a Jew living under a false identity in New York who claims to have heard that photographs of the pair were delivered to a counterfeit document maker. The interrogation is continuing, but I wanted you to be aware of the situation."

Archie pushed his plate away, "No more!" he said with a chuckle. "You've outdone yourself honey."

"That was a great dinner Mom," said Cindy echoing her father.

"Just wait 'til you try the dessert. Cindy, help me with the coffee," beamed Trish.

"Mom, can Karen come over this evening? Will you drive her home?" asked Mary.

"Sure. One of us can drive her home. Go give her a call."

Trish and Cindy came back in and set cup and saucers with steaming freshly brewed coffee on the table. "So what are you kids planning to do over spring break?" asked Trish.

"We've decided to drive south and see some of the countryside," said Rudy. "Neither of us has been to New Orleans, and I hear it's becoming more popular than Daytona Beach."

"Well that sounds like fun! Doesn't it dear?"

"How long will you be gone?" asked Archie.

"We'll be gone most of the time," said Cindy. "But we'll be back in time for classes."

Frank had woken up in the middle of the night and realized that it was quiet. He nudged his wife awake and said, "Listen."

"I don't hear anything."

"Yep. The cows have quit calling their calves. Something's wrong."

Frank and Marge pulled on their clothes, grabbed a flashlight, and headed out to the barnyard.

Marge said, "Where's Lady?"

When they got to the barn they saw immediately what was going on. All the calves were back with their mothers and lying contentedly at their feet.

"I'll be damned," said Frank.

Miriam and Levi were leaning against the fence. Lady was sitting with them.

Frank and Marge walked over and leaned against the fence next to them.

"They can't stay with their moms, Miriam," said Frank. "We'll have to separate them again in the morning."

"No," said Miriam. "I won't let you."

"You won't let us?"

"No. The cows want their babies."

"We'll talk more about this in the morning," said Marge, nodding her head slightly to her husband.

"All right. Let's all go in. It's too chilly to be out here."

The next day when Frank began separating the cows and calves again, Miriam interfered. She wouldn't let him close the gates; she opened gates and pulled down the wire fences in front of the calf hutches. She was screaming and running around disrupting everything Frank did. Finally, Frank and Marge had to manhandle her into the house. They locked her into the secret room.

Levi stood by, unsure what he should do. He almost worshiped Frank and tried to be like him and do the things Frank did around the farm. But his first and strongest allegiance and attachment was unquestioningly to Miriam. Only moments after they had locked her into the room, Levi had let her out and once again she had headed to the barnyard to defend the cows and the calves.

"You're Germans!" she was shouting. She was beside herself and in a complete frenzy.

Frank and Marge finally sat down on a bale of hay.

"This can't go on," said Frank. "What are we going to do?"

"I don't think she's going to get over this," said Marge. "I don't think she's going to let us separate them. We can't keep her locked up. I don't even know if we could. Levi wouldn't let us. Maybe they need to go somewhere else."

Rebbe Shrinkle was again sitting on the park bench watching his son and other children playing. He was glancing through a newspaper.

A woman with a young girl walked into the playground. They stood and talked for a moment. The girl ran to the swings and the woman walked over to the bench.

"Do you mind if I sit here?"

"Of course not," said the Rebbe.

She opened a small paper bag and pulled out a cellophane-wrapped pastrami sandwich that she leisurely unwrapped and took a bite of. She swallowed and wiped her mouth with a paper napkin. "Leon Miller has been picked up," she said into her napkin.

The Rebbe sat quietly, contemplating the ramifications of this news. Leon had been part of the community for a long time. He had recently helped get documents to the forger for the two lab Jews. It was possible that he would reveal the forger's name.

"How long ago?" asked the Rebbe quietly to no one in particular.

The woman finished another bite of her sandwich and wiped her mouth. "Six days."

Rebbe Shrinkle was more alarmed. If it had been a mistake, or if Leon's papers had been accepted as genuine, he would have been released in only a day or two. He had to assume that Leon's ancestry had been discovered. Maybe they had broken him. The Rebbe tried to calculate the ramifications. Although Leon was only a part of a chain, and he did not know many of the people along the way, he did know the document maker. This could be catastrophic. He knew that few people could resist torture for very long. Leon would probably reveal everything he knew.

Rebbe Shrinkle tried to keep a note of calm reassurance in his voice, "We must abandon the meeting place for now. Everyone should be told to prepare to hide if need be. We will get through this. We must be calm. Be brave and pray." He stood up and called his son over to him. "Let's go home Benny!"

Cindy was waiting in their small green Volkswagen sedan when Rudy finished his final class of the term. The car was packed for a road trip; the tank was full. He got in on the passenger side, leaned over and kissed Cindy hello. They headed out of town, but instead of heading south toward New Orleans, they drove southeast along the Illinois River retracing the route taken by Frank Lutz just over a year earlier.

The sun was setting. The sky was filled with a blazing red and orange sunset when they drove slowly into the farm and parked next to the white van with the faded carpet cleaning logo they both remembered well. As they got out of the car, a man came out of the house. A black and white dog who was clearly on alert stood close to him. "Can I help you?" he asked.

"I recognize the woman," called Marge, stepping out of the house.

"Welcome," said Frank, offering his hand. "It's ok Lady," he said reaching down and patting the dog. "Come in."

They stepped through the back door and into a large kitchen. Marge walked over to the stove and wrapped on the wall next to it. A moment later Miriam and Levi walked cautiously into the kitchen. They were each carrying a small suitcase and had a backpack over one shoulder.

Rudy and Cindy were shocked at the transformation. These two people looked nothing like the two creatures they helped escape. That filthy, pale, and cowering couple had been replaced.

"Miriam?" said Cindy.

Miriam was wearing a pair of jeans and a long-sleeve pale red flannel shirt. Her sneakers were grass-stained. Her dark hair was pulled back and tied behind her head.

Miriam walked to Cindy and held out her hand, "I don't know your name," she said.

"I'm Patty," she lied. "You look so good!" She gave Miriam a hug. "And Levi?" she said. "Look at you!"

"They've done really well here," said Marge.

"We hate seeing them go," said Frank, "But they won't stay."

"What's the problem?" asked Rudy.

"We have to go now," said Levi. "Can you take us?"

"Yes, we're going to take you somewhere else," said Rudy, "but maybe we can work this out."

"No," said Miriam. "Now."

"Well, I guess we can go now," said Cindy looking at the man and woman as Miriam and Levi walked past them and out the back door.

Frank shrugged and followed them out.

Cindy opened the trunk and helped them stow their bags. She opened the back door for them and Miriam got in quickly. Levi squatted down in front of Lady. He put his arms around her neck as she licked his face. He stood up; his eyes were tearing. He gave Marge a long hug and then offered his hand to Frank.

Frank pulled Levi close in a tight embrace and let him go. Levi got into the car next to Miriam.

"All right then. I guess we're leaving," said Rudy with more than a bit of confusion in his voice. He shook Frank and Marge's hand, got in the car and said, "Let's go honey."

Cindy shook their hands and got in and closed the door. Rudy started the engine. Frank leaned in through the open back window and said, "You both have a home here if you ever need it. Levi?"

"I know. Thanks," said Levi. "Thanks for everything, we'll never forget you and Marge."

"Miriam?" said Frank.

Miriam looked at him for a moment. "Thank you," she said. "Let's go now."

Charles Hampton was an aging commercial artist. He drew images for two advertising firms. He had illustrated seventeen children's books and he had forged hundreds of documents proving that people had descended from long lines of Aryan relatives.

Every night for the past fifty-three years, Hampton had carefully set the hidden trip switch on the door jam. He had done this religiously. The blank documents he kept hidden in his studio were valuable and would probably send him to prison forever if they were discovered, but the meticulously researched genealogy records he used when filling out the blank forms would expose hundreds of people and their families to grave possibilities if the authorities got a hold of them.

The trip switch was attached to a wire that led to a series of charges he had hidden under the floorboards, behind the paneling, and in the ceiling. He had designed it so that if someone opened the door unexpectedly, and to do so they would have to break the three locks he always clicked into place, the entire studio would almost immediately erupt into flame and every record would be destroyed.

But the charges had been set half a century earlier. Over the decades a few mice had passed through. One stayed over one winter and took a liking to the insulation on the wires. Her nibbling habit didn't destroy the system, but when the Orpo burst through the door, the explosions were fewer and the resulting flames not as intense as Charles had planned.

The bomb under Charles' bed was one that still worked perfectly however; he was killed in his sleep. The genealogy records were hidden between the mattress and the box springs. The Orpo agents were able to quell many of the fires with old throw rugs that filled the little apartment and studio. The bedroom was burning with intensity when the fire engine arrived and hosed it down.

The mattress and box springs had insulated the records to a degree. They were badly charred but the forensic agents were meticulous with every scrap of paper they found and duly preserved them for later analysis.

They had driven all night. They had stopped twice and filled their car with gas. Cindy and Rudy took turns driving and they pressed on.

The sun was coming up. Levi and Miriam had their faces close to the windows and were staring out at the changing scenery.

"Let's stop at the next rest stop," said Rudy. It's late enough that there shouldn't be a lot of cars there. I need to pee. Anyone else?"

A few miles later, he pulled off the highway. It wasn't much; a small kiosk with a drink and candy machine and two concrete block restrooms. Only one other car was there, but it was pulled to the far end of the parking lot. Someone was in the grassy area next to it walking a dog on a leash.

When Miriam and Cindy got back to the car, Miriam asked, "How much longer?"

"Another 12 hours, maybe less," said Rudy. "Let me show you the map." He traced his finger along the route they had come and along their future path to a small town in central Texas. "This is where we're going. My parents own a cabin on a river. It's pretty secluded. You'll be safe there for a while. Someone's trying to find a better place for you; this is just a temporary place."

"You guys want another sandwich?" asked Cindy.

"Sure," said Levi.

"By the way, my name isn't Patty, it's Cindy. I didn't want them to know our real names."

Tell Me Your Story

As they sped along in their small car, the flat unbroken landscape was changing. For a while, it was dominated by rows of corn and soybeans, then wheat, oats and rye took over, cotton and sorghum replaced the grains, and finally, it was all hay. But then, the unbroken flat expanse began to undulate and stone outcroppings began to appear. The air turned drier and the farm fields disappeared altogether. The ground looked stony and comparatively barren as the sage, oak, and mesquite replaced the cultivated fields. Steepening hills began making the car work harder while dabs of bright colors started to grow into broad swaths.

"It's amazing isn't it?" said Rudy. "The bloom here lasts only a few weeks, but people come from all over to take pictures and just look." They drove through an artist's pallet of swirling colors.

They turned off the highway and onto a narrow two-lane road that became all up and down. Steep hills slowed their pace, but they sped along the downhill sides. In the narrow ravines, small rivulets flowed, and prickly pear cactus signaled that the water was only seasonal.

"Usually," said Rudy, "there's no water at all in these draws. This is dry country."

Twice, as they hurdled down a steep slope they had to slow quickly near the bottom as herds of goats crossed the road. "These goats are really wild. They were released centuries ago. They call them Spanish goats because they were brought here by the early Spanish explorers."

The road flattened a bit and Rudy stopped in front of a rude barbed wire gate. "Cindy, why don't you drive, we have a few more gates we have to go through. We have to go slow the rest of the way." He opened the gate and closed it behind them after she had driven through.

Twice more, they turned onto ever smaller, more rocky, less traveled tracks, until finally, he said they were there.

The road, if it could be called a road, led downward until finally coming to a house set on a wide but shallow river. It was an unpainted rustic affair with a gray corrugated metal roof splotched with a few spots of red rust. A large screened in porch wrapped all the way around. "I'll show everyone around, and then I'm taking a long nap."

After weeks of painstaking recovery and careful preservation the charred remains of Charles Hampton's genealogy records, the documents he had futilely given his life to try and keep out of the government's hands, were yielding many family names. The names had been cross-referenced in the massive Central North American Reich Command's racial history database and resulted in a list of over three thousand individuals whose records claimed that they were descendants of these Aryan lines.

North American Oberstgruppenführer Heinz Schimmelpfennig had reviewed the records and the summary report. He had copies sent to his senior staff. He instructed them to do nothing with the information for the time being since the case had, naturally, been turned over to the Death Heads, the Gestapo Totenkopfs.

The cabin was a split-level built on the side of the hill running down to the river. Two bedrooms, a small bathroom, and a large den with a stone fireplace made up the upper level. The lower level had another bedroom, another bathroom, a dining room, and a remarkably large kitchen. As they walked around the cabin, the dark corners in the eaves and the ceiling seemed to be filled with dark cobwebs, but when Miriam reached out and touched one, it scattered into a myriad of little rods and undulating brown pencil eraser-sized bodies scurrying a short distance. Levi gasped loudly at the effect.

Rudy laughed and explained that they were daddy-long-legs, a relative of spiders, but harmless. For the rest of the day, Levi poked at each group of them he found.

After turning on the gas at the large propane tank, and lighting the large chest freezer, the refrigerator, and hot water heater, Rudy finally went off to take a nap, everyone else unloaded the car. They had brought many loaves of bread, peanut butter, jelly, lots of canned goods, dried beans and rice, flour, sugar, salt, some spices, margarine, cooking oil, bath supplies, toilet paper, soap, and sundry other items that Miriam and Levi would rely on while they were at the cabin. Rudy's parents had stocked the house with a large supply of canned goods and other supplies as well.

Once the supplies were stowed away, Cindy suggested that they go down to the river.

They walked down the gentle slope along a path overgrown with rank grass. The river was wide and strewn with large rocks. It was shallow but flowed swiftly. Cindy sat down on a flat gray rock and began talking off her shoes and socks. She looked over her shoulder and saw Miriam and Levi standing close together staring at the river.

"Is it really water?" asked Levi. "It's so big."

"Come on," called Cindy. "You'll like it. Take your shoes and socks off. Roll up your pants," she said, doing just that herself.

Cindy waded into the water. It came up to the middle of her calf. "Come on!"

Miriam led the way, pulling Rudy along by the hand. She sat down on the rock and began taking off her shoes.

"What are you doing?" demanded Levi. But she ignored him and pulled off her socks, rolled up her pants the way Cindy had, and stepped lightly into the water.

"Oh! It's nice," and followed Cindy.

"Watch this!" called Cindy, and all of a sudden she sat down in a small pool as the water rushed around her shoulders. Then she stood up so that they could see that the little pool was only waist deep. "Rudy calls them bathtubs. Come try it."

As Miriam inched her way closer, Cindy called, "Be a little careful. Right there. Do you see it? Get in and sit down." Miriam bravely did, and quickly, they were both laughing and saying things that Levi could no longer hear over the loud gurgling of the water as it splashed and hurried around the rocks. He began pulling off his shoes.

By the time Rudy and Cindy pulled out of the driveway to hurry back to Chicago, Miriam and Levi had been instructed about everything Rudy could think of that might happen to them and that they might need. There was plenty of food, Levi had learned to be reasonably handy in the kitchen when they were at the farm, and the propane would last at least six months. They had come up with a cover story in the unlikely event that someone stopped by. In the decade or so that his parents had owned the house, Rudy couldn't remember one time when anyone had shown up unexpectedly. The widely scattered neighboring houses were seldom-used vacation getaways. He thought, and told them that more people might be around in the fall when deer hunting season started, but they hoped to have found them a more permanent home before then. Everyone hug, shook hands, and suddenly, Miriam and Levi were on their own.

Rudy and Cindy drove back without stopping for anything but gas. They got back late Saturday night and collapsed into bed. They slept in until almost noon. Rudy got up, started the coffee, and grabbed the Sunday paper that had been delivered to their door.

"Oh my God," he said, reading the headlines as he crawled back into bed.

Cindy sat up, still groggy and tired from the long trip, "What is it?"

"47 Jews Discovered by Gestapo," he said, reading the headlines to her.

It was almost as bad as Rebbe Shrinkle had feared it could be. He had heard that many people were being arrested; entire families were being taken. Every time he learned a new name, he whispered the Av Harachamim to himself and asked God to give them the courage and strength to die a martyr. But he knew that most of them were just ordinary people who would not be able to withstand the Nazis for long. He had no misconceptions of what they might be going through, but could barely make himself imagine the details of what they were enduring.

Trish sat alone at the dining room table reading the front page story. Her coffee cup was still full and the slice of cherry pie on the Delft dessert plate was missing only one bite. She was halfway through the story of the Gestapo catching the Jews. When she began reading she had gotten quite angry that Jews had been pretending to be good ordinary people. It reinforced her low opinion of them and her belief that they couldn't be trusted. But as she read on, she saw the name of a friend of hers. The records that the Gestapo had recovered from the fire had led them to cities all over North America, even to Chicago. At first she thought it must be a mistake, or a coincidence of similar names, but no, it was clear that the article was talking about the same Dr. and Mrs. Gerald Brownstone who had been playing bridge with her and Archie only two weeks earlier. Emily Brownstone was one of her best friends, maybe her best friend. Their daughters had grown up together. Yet there it was in black and white. The Brownstones were Jews, pretending to be good Caucasians, just like the Nelsons.

At first she felt betrayed, but those feeling evaporated quickly as she began to imagine what was happening to her friend; in spite of herself, she realized that she still thought of her as a friend, and someone she cared about very deeply. As she read through the article she kept reading about "interrogations" of the prisoners, and the effort to get them to reveal the names of other Jews; she wasn't hungry any longer and wanted badly to talk to Archie, but he had been called into work unexpectedly.

Archie began to sweat.

There was a man neatly dressed in a dark business suit waiting for him in his office when he arrived. He stood immediately and introduced himself as Detective Mengersen. He had a casual smile on his face and offered his hand. The overhead light glinted off the small silver skull and crossbones on his lapel. Archie took his hand, noting the man's limp cold grip.

"What can I do for you detective? The phone message from my secretary said it was an urgent matter."

"There was more urgency an hour ago, but some urgency remains, and you will be needed for the rest of the day."

"I don't understand, is there a problem in the colony?"

"No, no. I'm sure your subjects are in perfect health. As you may have heard, we have picked up a number of Jews around the country; we were able to catch nine of them here in Chicago. We know how Jews operate, eh Dr. Nelson? We believe they know the names and whereabouts of other Jews hiding around the country.

"Unfortunately, they are too stupid to know what is good for them, and we have lost a few who have insisted on staying quiet.

"We need your help keeping them alive, to help us with our interrogations; sometimes our technicians become a little too, how should I put it, uh, exuberant in their work. I'm sure you understand."

Archie could feel the sweat from his armpit begin to trickle coldly down his side.

Every eye in the Rathskeller was on the two students. No one was drinking or eating; the student workers behind the counter had stopped serving beer and snacks. The conversation had risen suddenly in volume and intensity.

A petite coed with her dark hair cropped stylishly short was now yelling at a much larger male student who was flushing a brighter red each passing moment. Even from across the room where Rudy and Cindy were sitting, a fine spray of saliva could be seen flying from her mouth as she screamed at the boy.

"Brinker is the best professor on this campus! Who gives a shit if he's a Jew? We're here to learn, not to crucify people!" She was visibly shaking; her nose was flared and they could hear her harsh inhale.

But her opponent was not ready to give ground it seemed. His bulk dwarfed her. Rudy thought he might recognize him from the wrestling team. "We don't want dirty Jews here! They lie and stink! We're Germans! Aryans should teach Aryans! Fuck you! You're probably a secret Jew too!" And with that he pushed her aside and marched out of the beer hall yelling, "Sieg Heil!"

The young woman was crying and looking around. Her chest was heaving. "What's wrong with you people? Does it really matter if professor Brinker is a Jew? He's the best teacher on campus and now he's probably being tortured just because his grandparents were Jewish! Wake up!" Sobbing, she gathered her books and papers and hurried out.

Archie followed the Gestapo detective into a bleak concrete room in the basement. Another room was connected to it. There was a window in the wall between the two rooms. There was a naked man on his back tied to a table in the center of the room. The foot end of the table was raised up, its legs on top of two thick telephone books. The man was sobbing between gasps. Two men dressed in lab coats stood on each side of him and looked up as the detective and Archie entered the room.

"Heil Hitler!" one of the men shouted, and they both snapped to attention. Detective Mengersen nodded to them.

"Any luck?" he asked casually.

"No Detective. He swears he isn't a Jew."

Archie recognized the man on the table as soon as he had stepped into the room. He looked through the window and saw Emily Brownstone and her daughter Julia along with five other people he didn't know hanging by their wrists from a steam pipe that ran across the room just below the ceiling. Their clothes had been taken from them. There seemed to be some acknowledgement in their eyes when they saw him, but his close friend, Dr. Jerry Brownstone didn't seem to recognize him, which Archie thought was probably a good thing.

"Carry on,' ordered Mengersen. "Dr. Nelson is here in case of another accident." He nodded at Archie and motioned toward a body slumped in a corner. "Take good care of our Jews, doctor." He walked out closing the door behind him.

One of the two technicians grabbed Jerry's shoulders and shouted at him. "Who is a Jew?"

Jerry was crying and protesting. "Why are you doing this? I'm not a Jew; I don't know any Jews."

One of the technicians put a wet towel over Jerry's face. The other one picked up a bucket of water and poured it over his face. Jerry struggled and gasped. Through the window, everyone in the other room could see what was happening. They finally pulled the towel off his face, and began shouting at him again. Jerry could only gasp and sob.

One of the techs said something quietly that Archie could not quite catch. "We will be right back doctor," one of them said to him, and then they left the room.

Archie felt his friend's pulse; it was racing of course. He lifted his eyelids and checked his pupils. Jerry seemed to be on the verge of shock. He went to the connecting door and into the other room. He made a quick visual inspection of everyone hanging by their wrists. One of them seemed to have a dislocated shoulder, and most of their hands were beginning to swell. They were bruised and clearly in serious distress.

He stopped between Emily and Julia and said quietly to them, "I'll try to get you out, but I don't know about Jerry; I'll try. Be brave."

Archie stepped back through the door just as the two technicians came back in.

"This man is on the verge of shock. Don't touch him until I get back. That's an order!" He left and hurried to his office. He didn't know whether he had the authority to order the inquisitors to do anything; he hoped that the "accident" and Mengersen's order that he take care of the prisoners would give him a little leverage.

In his office he put together a kit with supplies he imagined would make it look like he was going to assist the technicians: I.V. bags of saline and lines, needles, vials of various drugs. At the same time he put together a box of medical supplies he thought he and his family might need. He picked up the phone and called his wife.

"Hi honey. It's me."

"Have you seen the paper? And about the Brownstones?"

"Yes. That's why I'm calling. They're here. I'm going to try and get them out. Listen carefully and do exactly what I say; I don't have time to explain. Call the kids; have them come to the house right away. Don't let Mary go anywhere. Go to the bank and take out as much as they allow. Put suitcases together for... well, we might never get back home. Do you understand?"

"What do you mean 'never get back home'?"

"There's no time now. Call the kids; tell Mary to stay home, go to the bank. Be ready to leave as soon as we get there. I love you." He hung up and hurried back to the interrogation rooms. Along the way he grabbed a stack of lab scrubs, some shoe covers, and a rolling laundry hamper half filled with dirty linens.

Trish hung up the phone and had a second bite of pie. She stared out the window at the tree limbs swaying gently in the light early summer breeze. She took a sip of her now-cool coffee, and looked again at her friends' names in the newspaper. She took a deep breath and let out a long sigh. Then she picked up the phone and called her daughter.

Archie entered the room with his bag of medical tools. The techs were slapping Jerry and screaming in his face.

"I ordered you to leave that man alone! Detective Mengersen will hear about this."

The techs glanced at each other. "We thought you meant just the water-boarding, Herr Doctor. We would not go against your orders."

Archie set the bag of supplies on a table. He took out his stethoscope and listened to Jerry's heart. He shook his head. "We need to use someone else. By now the others must see what is in store for them if they don't cooperate."

The two techs looked at each other again and nodded. "Let's have the girl next," said the taller one. "We can play with her."

"First let me give this one an injection. I'll give the girl one too when we switch them." Archie went to his bag of supplies and drew up two large syringes full of Ketamine, and then went over to Jerry, a syringe in both hands. "Help me here," he ordered. "Unstrap him, and roll him over."

The two technicians hurried to comply, and once the straps were off, they stood together and reached across Jerry and began to roll him over.

Archie walked up behind them quickly and plunged a needle deep into the base of their necks. He pushed the large dose of the powerful anesthetic into each of them. They jerked back, and grabbed at the syringes still stuck in their necks. They turned, glanced at each other and then at Archie, confusion in their eyes and on their faces.

"What, why, did…" began one of them, and then they both collapsed on the floor. They would be unconscious for hours with a dose the size he had just given them. Archie hoped he hadn't killed them.

He grabbed the hamper from outside the door and grabbed the pale green scrubs. He then manhandled the two inquisitors into it. He covered them with the dirty towels and sheets inside.

He went to Jerry and turned his head so that they were looking at each other. "Jerry! It's me, Archie. Pull yourself together. Sit up! We have to hurry."

He grabbed a heavy pair of scissors and a chair and hurried into the next room, leaving Jerry on the table. He rushed from person to person, stood on the chair, cut the plastic ties around their wrists and lowered them to the floor. "Hurry!" he told them, "There are scrubs in the other room. Put them on. Hurry!" When he cut down Emily he told her to help with Jerry.

Finally, with much moaning and confused expressions, everyone but one woman was dressed. She was still naked and sitting next to the dead man in the corner holding him and crying.

Archie went over and tried to get her into a uniform, but she seemed inconsolable. "We have to go now. We can't wait for you. Please come." But she seemed not to hear him; he knew he didn't have the time to argue with her.

"Listen everyone. I don't know if we can make it out, but we're gong to try. You must listen carefully and do exactly as I say. I can't help you with your wrists right now, but please try to be quiet. This is our only chance. Wait here."

Archie left the room and looked up and down the hallway. In this part of the sub-basement, most of the rooms were used for storage; few people were around. He walked quickly to the elevator and called it. After what seemed an eon, it arrived and the door opened. No one was inside. Archie leaned in and pushed the stop elevator button, and then hurried back to the room.

"Lets go!" he ordered, and glanced one last time at the woman holding her dead husband. He was sorry she wouldn't let him try to help her.

Out they hurried and into the waiting elevator.

"We're going up only one level. We have to go down a long hall to get to the parking garage, where my car is. If we see anyone just act like you belong here."

The elevator door opened but no one else was in the hallway. No one stopped them as they made their way to the garage and into Archie's car. He drove about two miles from the hospital and pulled into an apartment project parking lot. He had seen clothes hanging on a line and figured that this was as good as any place else he could drop them.

He turned off the engine and looked at the four people crammed in the back.

"These people are my friends," he said motioning to the Brownstones, crammed in the front seat with him. "I have to let the rest of you out here; there's nothing more I can do for you. There're clothes hanging on a line over there. Get them."

He pulled out his wallet and gave them all the money he had.

"There isn't anything else I can do for you. None of us might be able to escape. Listen, it might be better to end your lives than to have them catch you again. Good luck. Now, I'm sorry, but get out of the car."

They sat still for a moment, in their green lab outfits, each holding a few dollars. They were confused and unsure of what to do.

"Get out!" yelled Archie, and got out and pulled a back door open and pulled them out. Everyone was crying and hugging each other. "Hurry! Get some clothes. Try to call someone who can help you. I'm sorry."

He slammed the door and got back in. "Emily, you and Julia get in back now."

They did, and he sped off, leaving the other four people standing in the parking lot.

Rudy and Cindy came through the door. "Mother!" she yelled.

"I'm right here," said Trish hurrying down the stairs. Mary was behind her, clearly worried.

"We saw the article. It mentioned the Brownstones."

"I saw it too," she said, and repeated the phone message she had gotten from her husband.

Just then the backdoor opened and Archie came in leading the Brownstones. "Oh Em," said Trish rushing to her friend. "They're saying you're a Jew."

"I am a Jew, Patricia. So is Jerry. I'm sorry we could never tell you the truth."

"Patricia," thought Trish. They had been Em and Trish since before the girls were born. She sensed that Em expected her to see her differently now, to treat them like Jews. She had always defended the Reich's efforts; she had always believed what they said, that the Jews were dirty, liars, swindlers, and only out to rob their neighbors and undermine the government. She had been taught to think of them as subhumans and had spoken often about the Jewish problem with Em. Now, though, come to think of it, she wondered whether it might have been her doing most of the talking in those conversations. It took only a moment's reflection for her to completely change her mind. All at once she saw the lies behind the government's propaganda of hate.

She looked squarely into her friend's eyes and said, "Please call me Trish, Em. I don't care if you are a Martian. You need some clothes."

"We don't have much time," said Archie. He explained briefly what he had done and why they had to leave right away. "It won't be long until they guess that I'm involved somehow, the police will be here pretty soon, even if it's just to ask me what I know.

89

"Rudy, do you think you and Cindy will be all right if you stay behind? I wanted to give you the chance of leaving with us."

Rudy and Cindy looked at each other. "I'd be worried that they would use Cindy somehow to lure you back or to trap you some how. We're all involved now, I think. I don't see how we can stay. Cindy?"

Cindy put her arm around Rudy's waist and put her head on his chest. She looked up at her father. "We should probably try to get to Rudy's parents' cabin. There's a lot of supplies there."

North American Oberstgruppenführer Heinz Schimmelpfennig picked up the phone in his den to take a call from the Gestapo Totenkopf detective. He was surprised that he was being disturbed at home on a Sunday, but the duty officer had called ahead and told him that the detective had said it was absolutely urgent and was given permission to pass along Schimmelpfennig's private number. He was relishing the likely news of some extraordinary breakthrough from the interrogations in Chicago.

"Yes detective?"

Detective Mengersen rolled the small silver death head pin on his lapel absently between his thumb and middle finger. He had never had to report such a large blunder before. He knew that this might cost him his job and perhaps much more.

"Sieg Heil, Oberstgruppenführer Schimmelpfennig. I'm sorry to disturb you on a Sunday, but I thought you needed to know what has happened right away."

Schimmelpfennig could tell that Mengersen had not called with good news.

"What is it detective?"

"All but two of the Jews we had in Chicago are gone. We are trying to determine what happened to them, but it appears that someone helped them. Two junior-grade officers were assaulted. A doctor who was helping with the interrogation is missing as well. We believe he might have been taken as a hostage."

"You still have two of them?"

"Only one, Herr Oberstgruppenführer. One is dead. A man. He might have been killed during the escape," he lied. "But we have his wife. She seems to know nothing and is almost incoherent—a typical Jewess."

Schimmelpfennig sighed loudly. From the next room, his wife recognized the sound of his deep irritation. He knew that Berlin would not be happy with this turn of events. Jews don't escape. He worried about how the story would be covered in the media. As much as he could, he would try to put the blame on the Gestapo. Their people had lost the prisoners. They should be the ones trying to get them back. If they couldn't, well, maybe Mengersen had some Jewish blood somewhere in his background, who knows?

"See to it that they are found detective. Keep me informed." And with that, he hung up.

Mengersen knew that he was being set up as a scapegoat, but at least he was still working, and at least had a chance at some sort of redemption; but he would have to find the missing Jews and the doctor.

It took longer than Archie had hoped, but they were finally away from the house. He was driving their dark blue Audi. Mary was in the back seat with her mother and Emily Brownstone. Jerry was riding shotgun.

Behind them, though far enough away that it wasn't obvious that they were following them, were Rudy, Cindy, and Julie Brownstone in their small green Volkswagen. They had a set of two-way radios that Mary had gotten for Christmas two years earlier but hadn't played with very much. One was in each car. Archie had wanted everyone to leave their cell phones behind, worried that they might be easily tracked, but at Rudy's suggestion, they kept his and Cindy's, but pulled out the batteries and buried them in the trunk under all their other gear to shield any possible signal from them.

He pulled off the highway at the exit to the airport. Rudy followed more closely as they drove into and parked in short-term parking. Rudy pulled up and parked next to the Audi.

"Cindy, you girls wait here in our car. Rudy and I'll be right back."

When they returned and had switched cars again, Julie asked where they had gone.

"We went to long-term parking and drove around until we found a dark blue Audi like Dr. Nelson's. It might even have been the same year. We switched license plates. The longer it takes the owners of the other car to come home and to notice the change, the longer we can drive without too much worry at being caught. We snagged a replacement plate for our car too."

Tell Me Your Story

The Gestapo's investigation revealed almost right away that Archie had not been a victim. Surveillance videos in the basement and parking garage had shown him leading a group of seven scrub-clad people out of the building. An alert had been sent to all the police agencies in the Chicago area.

Mengersen took three agents with him when he went to the Nelsons'. There did not appear to be anyone home, so they forced the door and searched the house. It was obvious from the clothes on the bed and the empty kitchen cupboards that the Nelsons were running. The neighbors had not noticed anything going on and were of no help.

Mengersen went back to Archie's office and began reviewing his personnel file for possible leads on where he might have gone. He sent agents to a brother's home in Milwaukee, his wife's mother's apartment in Joliet, and the Nelson's vacation cabin on Michigan's upper peninsula.

The brother and the mother had not heard from him and had no knowledge of his whereabouts. The agents who interrogated them were sure they were not withholding any information; the questioning had been thorough. A helicopter had been dispatched to the cabin, but it was empty. Megersen ordered that a watch be maintained on all three locations; wiretaps were standard procedure.

When Mengersen interviewed the senior staff at Joseph Mengele Memorial Hospital for Genetic and Racial Disease, he learned from Chief of Staff Eckel that Archie had been hired as the medical director of the subhuman colony because his daughter had married into the main Master Race line. Her husband's parents were highly respected upper administrators with the North American Reich Command in Chicago.

This information gave Mengersen more than a moment's pause. His career, and maybe more he feared, was already in grave danger because of the escape; it might be immediate suicide to start questioning Nelson's daughter, Cynthia Maria Schwartz, and he was even less happy over the possible results of questioning her husband, Rudolph Hess Schwartz. Still, her father had disappeared. Mengersen might be able to ask her a few polite questions about his possible whereabouts without appearing to be accusing her of anything; but if he didn't question her, his superiors would accuse him of incompetence. It was a dilemma.

After a few hours, Mengersen decided that he didn't really have a choice. He simply had to capture Dr. Nelson if he had any hope of survival; getting the Jews back as well would be even better insurance.

He called their apartment, but all he got was their machine. He left a very polite message and asked them to call him at their convenience.

He called back the next day, and as politely as he had ever done before, explained that he needed to speak with Mrs. Schwartz on urgent police business concerning her father.

He still hadn't heard back the next day, so went to the university and waited for her outside her classroom. But she didn't come out. When the professor came out, Mengersen asked him whether Mrs. Schwartz had last been to class on Monday; she hadn't.

Mengersen was more worried. If he couldn't reach Cynthia Schwartz, he might be forced to speak with her husband. He realized once again that circumstances were forcing him down a path he had hoped to avoid. With misgivings, he got directions to the Political Science department's office, and walked across the campus worrying how he would broach this sensitive matter with Schwartz.

The day Rudy and Cindy had driven away Miriam and Levi were on their own for the first time. Never before hadn't there been someone to tell them what to do. Even on the farm, there had usually been watchful eyes on them and gentle directions about when and where to do what.

As the small car drove out of sight, they glanced over at each other at the same time with questions in their eyes.

"Do you think they'll come back?" said Levi.

"I don't know," answered Miriam, "but we should plan what we are going to do whether they come back or not."

"What do you mean? What can we do?"

"We could leave," said Miriam. "We have our papers. Maybe we could go farther away. I saw a book like the one we had at Frank and Marge's. It's filled with maps. Rudy showed us on his map where we are and where we drove. I think I understand them. We could try to find the wild places like we saw on TV, where there aren't people. If they catch us, they'll take us back to the lab."

Rudy was dazed by Miriam's words. He was more confused than Miriam by all the dramatic and sudden changes in their lives.

"We should go?"

"Not now. Maybe later. Let's think. Let's be ready."

Over the few days that they were alone, they had been able to figure out many things about their new home. They spent hours each day in the river and walking along the shore looking at the small fish and bugs. Miriam made them sneak along very quietly to discover what was jumping into the water. From books in the house they learned that the animals they were seeing were frogs and crayfish.

In their explorations they followed a deer trail leading from the river that passed by a small rock outcropping that formed a small cave. Miriam remembered Frank's careful attention to a place for them to hide. They filled two pillowcases with supplies and hauled them and a plastic garbage can to the little cave. Within a day they had it stocked with food, clothes, and water. Miriam made them keep another bag ready, for the few items she thought they should take, but didn't want to leave at the cave.

They ate when they wanted, mostly peanut butter and jelly sandwiches and ice water. Rudy cooked rice and warmed a can of beans. Miriam made them eat outside; neither one of them seemed able to get enough sky and clouds and sun. At night, they laid together on a blanket looking up at the moon and stars.

On the first night, Rudy curled up on a couch, and Miriam crawled into one of the beds; but after about an hour, Rudy got into bed with Miriam.

"I don't like to be alone."

"Stay here. I was going to get on the couch with you." After that first night, they always slept together.

It was very late one night, about a week after Rudy and Cindy had driven off, that they awakened suddenly and heard the sound of a car. Headlights flashed quickly across their window from some distance away.

"Hurry!" ordered Miriam.

"Good afternoon. I would like to speak with Rudolph Hess Schwartz on an urgent matter of great importance," said Mengersen, showing his identification card to the secretary. The nameplate on her desk said, Helen Lomer, Department Secretary.

The death's head on his card made Lomer look at him with some suspicion. Though the regular police and even the SiPo were respected, many people believed the rumors of the Gestapo's cruelty. She liked Rudy; he had been a student in the department for five years. She had even attended his wedding to that lovely Chicago gal.

"What's this about, Detective?" she asked, relying on Rudy's Master Race membership to shield her from too much intimidation.

"This doesn't concern you, Miss Lomer. May I please speak with the department head?"

She thought for a moment about just saying no, but she knew she could only resist for so long.

"He's not here now, and he won't be back until early next week. He's at a conference in Denver.

"I would let you speak with Mr. Schwartz, he has a small office just down the hall. But he isn't here either; but I don't know where he is. He missed his Monday and his Wednesday class; a couple students called to ask whether the class had been officially cancelled. I don't know where he is."

Mengersen stood looking at her for a long moment.

"Detective?"

"Yes? Oh, yes. Thank you Miss Lomer. If he does come in, would you be so kind as to give him my card? Ask him to call me, please. This is an urgent matter."

Mengersen went back to Dr. Nelson's office. He argued with himself for a while. Should he call Schimmelpfennig for permission to search the Schwartz apartment? He was certain now that they had left at the same time as the girl's parents, with the Jews, but accusing Schwartz of being an accomplice in this despicable affair was dangerous; the idea that a German, someone named after a hero of the Reich would go so far, or could be so corrupted, good Aryans, members of the Master Race simply wouldn't throw everything away to help vermin. It was unthinkable. Yet, that was what seemed to have happened

Maybe the girl and her father had corrupted the boy's high ideals and strong morals? That was the safest way to explain the situation to Schimmelpfennig. He picked up the phone and made the call.

"Did you hear that?" asked Levi

"Shhh, be quiet." said Miriam.

They were huddled in their small cave, the bags already out of the garbage can and squeezed tightly in their fists.

"There it is again," whispered Levi.

"I don't hear anything, what is it?"

"I think someone is calling us. There. I think it's Rudy. Let's go see."

"No! Wait!" ordered Miriam. "Think first. Someone might be trying to fool us. It might be Germans." She thought for a moment. "Ok, we'll leave everything here and walk up the river and cross over and sneak up to the house until we know for sure. We must be very quiet."

As they made their way up the river, they came closer and closer to the house. Miriam heard them calling from the other side.

"You're right. It's them, but there are other voices too. We must be careful."

It took them about an hour to move in as slowly as Miriam demanded. Finally, they were able to see everyone clearly. Rudy was standing in the yard with his arms folded across his chest looking down the path to the river. Cindy was sitting on the steps with an older man. Another man and two older women were carrying bags from a dark blue car into the house. When Miriam saw the girl on the rope swing she took Rudy by the hand, sighed, and stepped out into the open.

"Rudy!" she called. "Here we are."

Cindy and Rudy ran over to them.

"We thought we must have scared you. We could tell you had run out in a hurry. We were worried that you might have just kept running."

"We almost did," smiled Levi. "Who are these people?"

Rick Bogle

The Fifth Part

After brief introductions all around, Rudy announced that he was going back.

"A few gas stops back, I dug out a phone and called my father. The authorities probably already know that Cindy and I have disappeared as well. They'll be contacting my parents; if they are asked where I might have gone, it's natural that they would think of the cabin. I asked my father to avoid saying anything at all until I spoke with him. He agreed, but he said it has to be in person. He wouldn't listen to any argument; so I have to go home.

"We talked this over in the car. We think Cindy should stay here. I'm going to explain to my parents what has happened and why. I think they'll understand, but I don't really know. I don't think we ever had any serious family discussions about Jews, so I don't know what they'll do. If Cindy isn't there, they can't turn her in.

"Put the batteries in the other phone every day for five minutes at exactly five PM. If you don't hear from me by Tuesday, four days from now, assume that you need to run. You'll need to leave immediately, but I'll do what I can to give you as much time as possible.

"Dr. Nelson?" said Rudy, looking for his opinion, "I don't know what else we can do. What do you think?"

"I don't like the idea of you leaving, and leaving without Cindy, but I think you're right. We'll have the phone on every day at five." Archie walked over to Rudy and gave him a big hug and said into his ear, "Please be careful Rudy."

Tell Me Your Story

North American Oberstgruppenführer Heinz Schimmelpfennig was himself a member of the Master Race. That gave him a certain freedom to question other members of the Race, but accusing a couple, both of whom held positions of some power, of having a son who had helped Jews escape was a serious matter. He would have liked to have left the investigation entirely in the hands of Gestapo Totenkopf detective Mengersen as a shield from possible recriminations, but the involvement of a member of the Race didn't make that possible.

Even after grilling Mengersen and being certain that the detective's conclusions were likely true, he hesitated to quickly question the Schwartzes. He need to be sure that no one would think he was being too aggressive. A few days shouldn't make too much of a difference.

The Schwartzes were aghast; they sat staring at Rudy wearing expressions he hadn't seen before. He had told them everything; how he and Cindy had snuck into Mengele and liberated Miriam and Levi; Dr. Nelson helping his friends and the others escape; and the fact that they were now hiding at the cabin.

"But honey," his mother began, "they're Jews. They're our enemies; they are parasites on the Fatherland. Why in the world would you want to be a part of all this?"

"Have you ever known a Jew, Mom?"

"Of course not. That's a silly question."

"But how do you know? The Schwartzes didn't know that the Brownstones were Jews. Mrs. Nelson hated the Jews as much as anyone I've known, even more than most. Yet Emily Brownstone was her best friend, someone she would do anything for, even help escape when it was discovered that she was a Jew.

"Maybe one of your friends is a Jew, and you just don't know it. I think Jews are just like us; they've being scapegoated by the Reich so that we all have a common enemy, not because they are a threat; how could they be a threat?"

"You're too young to remember the war, Rudy," his father said, "and I am too, but your great grandfather Heinz Wilhelm was there; the stories he told have been passed down to us. Everyone knows that the Jews were taking over the world before Hitler stepped in, that they had plans to enslave the gentiles, and that their religion condoned the sacrifice of gentile babies. Everyone knows this, and we know that the Jews had been trying to gain control for hundreds of years; domination, lying, cheating, it's in their genes Rudy; they can't change. The only thing we can do to survive is to exterminate them."

"But, Dad, can't you hear the propaganda in those words? I don't know how much of that stuff from history is true, but why couldn't they change? Why would they be the only race that has these genes? People from all over the world have married each other and have had kids who then married each other. And even if there are still pure Jews in the world, there must be so few of them that they simply couldn't be a threat to the Reich.

"And even if there is some threat, some secret cabal still plotting to take over the world, how does that justify what we are doing in the labs?"

"I don't know what you mean by that, Rudy," said his mother, "We have very strict laws governing the use of subhumans."

"Those laws don't mean very much. Look at this." He handed her the worn brochure he and Cindy first looked at in what seemed to him a lifetime ago: "Cruelty at RUC".

His mother visibly blanched when she opened it. She handed it to her husband.

"Rudy, this is just propaganda. Those pictures aren't real. Maybe they're from a long time ago, before the laws were put in place."

"I wish that was true," said Rudy quietly. "But Dr. Nelson says the whole thing's pretty accurate; it must be. That's the only thing that can explain why he would have risked so much or why he is risking the safety of his family.

"I've met two of the people who were being used in the labs. They were in the labs since they were young children. They have scars all over them; they were hurt repeatedly. The woman was raped repeatedly and then her babies were taken from her and experimented on. Do they deserve this simply because their great, great grand parents were bad people?"

"Even if these pictures are genuine, Rudy, and everything you are saying is true," began his father, "you have to put it in context. The two things you aren't considering are that medical progress would be stopped if we didn't experiment on subhumans, and aren't you being just a little too emotional about this? It isn't like subhumans are Germans or even Caucasians. They don't feel things like we do."

"But I have thought about those things. I've been reading a lot about all of this. This is exactly the same thing that scientists were saying about animals before we started breeding Jews and blacks for the labs. They said that if we stopped experimenting on animals that all medical progress would stop; but the more I read, the more I learned. It looks to me that nearly every advance has come about as a result of doctors studying their patients and trying new things when the old ones didn't work, and from scientists looking at and studying human ailments in human cells and tissues. The claims about animals were simply self-serving arguments from people trying to protect their careers.

"And so what if Jews don't feel things exactly the same way as Germans? Maybe men don't feel things the same way as women do, or old people the same way as young people. Our moral decisions have to be based on our similarities, not our differences, and it is simply inaccurate and a gross mistake to believe that the people in the labs aren't suffering just like you or I would if we were being treated the same way."

"I don't know what happened," said Cindy, "but it might have something to do with the burgers."

It had started the day after Rudy had left. Trish had brought hamburger, steaks, and a few other pieces of meat from their freezer at home. They had decided to make the most out of their circumstances and had fired up the barbecue grill.

Cindy, Miriam, Levi, Mary, and Julie Brownstone had been exploring the river, playing in the natural bathtubs and getting to know each other a little bit. Miriam liked showing Mary the things she and Levi had already discovered.

They were lounging in the warm water when they heard Mrs. Nelson calling them for lunch. When they got back to the cabin, they found the picnic table covered with a feast. There was even some fresh asparagus that Trish had found growing in a patch next to the house and a few early strawberries as well. In the middle of the table was a large platter of hot and still smoking hamburger patties just off the grill.

"I don't know how long we'll be able to stay here," said Archie, "but we might as well eat well while we can."

"Amen," said Jerry Brownstone, sitting down next to his wife. "Grab a burger before they get cold, everybody."

Levi looked across the table at Miriam and met her eyes looking at him. She got up from the table and walked off toward the river. Levi grabbed a couple of buns and the bowl of streaming asparagus and hurried to catch up with her.

"What in the world was that all about?" asked Emily Brownstone.

Cindy told them about the problems with the cows at the farm.

As soon as she finished, Mary suddenly stood up from the table and shouted, "Then I'm not eating them either!" and ran down the path to the river to find her new friends.

"We better go talk to them; they're probably in their cave."

They talked for three days. Everyone shared their stories. The Brownstones told about the difficulties and hardships of having to hide their heritage and beliefs from their friends and acquaintances while they were growing up. Julie Brownstone had been shocked when the family was arrested; she hadn't known that she was a Jew. Her parents explained that they had decided that it was best to keep the truth from her.

Cindy was embarrassed by the easy life she had led but she said she was proud of what she and Rudy had done for Miriam and Levi.

Archie talked about growing up in awe of the Race and hoping to become a doctor. He talked on and on about the things he had done in the colonies and how it had pulled the scales from his eyes; he said that rescuing his friends and the other Jews was the most important thing he had ever accomplished.

Trish Nelson sobbed through her story; she talked about how much she had hated Jews, about how embarrassed she was about the horrible things she must have said in front of her good friends, never knowing that she was really saying things that were completely untrue about them.

But when Levi and Miriam told their stories, stories they had practiced and told before, everyone else was stunned. Nothing had prepared them for the details of the torture, the deprivations, the rapes, the abuses, the fear, and the complete lack of morality and ethics inside the labs. Archie could only shake his head in agreement and corroboration when his family and friends looked over to see what his reaction was.

And every day at 5 PM they put the batteries in the phone and waited for Rudy's call. After three days, Cindy began to worry out loud.

"Something must be wrong," she said. "He would have called by now."

"He said to give him four days," said Archie. "We can trust him. Rudy's smart," he said, reassuring his daughter and everyone else. "He'll figure something out. He said his parents were good people."

Heinz Schimmelpfennig showed his identification card and was admitted to the lobby of Albert Speer Tower, the tallest building in Chicago, by a very polite doorman. He walked to the gold intercom and keyed in the Schwartz's apartment number.

"Yes?" came a woman's voice.

"Oberstgruppenführer Heinz Schimmelpfennig. I called earlier."

"Of course Herr Schimmelpfennig. Please come up."

Rudy was in a back room listening as his father answered the knock on the door and invited Schimmelpfennig into the apartment. He and his parents had agreed that they had to meet with Schimmelpfennig; refusing to do so would seem suspicious. He was in a bedroom just down a short hallway from the living room, and could hear what they were saying to each other. After some pleasantries, he heard his father invite the Oberstgruppenführer out onto the balcony. Why did he do that, Rudy wondered. Now he would have a hard time hearing what they were saying.

After a few minutes, he heard someone come back inside the apartment and walk down the hall. His mother opened the door and said, "Rudy, come into the living room, we have made a deal with the good Herr Schimmelpfennig."

"What? What do you mean a deal? We can't trust him," he said.

"He's Master Race too Rudy. Of course we can trust him. Come out sweetheart. He wants to talk to you."

Rudy was aghast. "We agreed that we'd just get him to go away!"

"Rudy! Come out here!" His father ordered from the other room.

"Come on, honey," said his mother, taking him by the hand and leading him into the living room."

"Sieg Heil!" said Schimmelpfennig reaching out his hand.

"What's this all about?"

"I've met with your parents Rudy. I had a long talk with your father last night on the phone. I think I understand the situation."

Rudy glared at his father. "What situation?"

"It seems that your wife has helped her father, Dr. Archibald Nelson, steal Jews. You understand that this is a crime of the highest order. It is a matter of the utmost importance. It places the national security at grave risk. We believe he is a Jewish sympathizer and may be planning a worldwide revolt. He must be captured and brought to trial, and then executed. The Jews he stole must be recovered for further questioning."

"I don't know where he is.

"Your parents have already explained everything to us Rudy. We have agents on the way to the cabin right now. Everyone will be caught. I guarantee it."

Rudy glanced at the clock on the mantle under the painting of his great grandfather. Cindy wouldn't have the phone on for another two hours.

"I helped Dr. Nelson. Cindy didn't know what I was doing."

"You are a true German, Rudy. Trying to take the blame and shield your wife is the honorable and brave thing to do, but I know everything you told your parents. She can't be saved. I'm sorry, but we can show no mercy to Nelson's family; they must be made an example.

"We have agreed that you were simply overcome by your wife's beauty and her father's propaganda. You are being sent back to Germany in the morning. I understand that you have many opportunities there with family. You will not be allowed to return to North America. I'm sorry Rudy, but it just won't do to have a member of the Race speaking out in the press or saying anything on behalf of the Jews."

Rudy knew he had to get away and stay free long enough to send Cindy and everyone else a warning. He bolted to the door, knocking a lamp over and pushing his father aside. He pulled the door open, but four uniformed Orpo officers were standing in the hall.

"One other thing Rudy," said the Oberstgruppenführer, "Did you actually think you were helping those two subhumans you got out of the lab? They don't know how to survive in the world; they were much better off in the lab where they could be taken care of properly. What you did was actually very cruel; how can you say you cared about them at all?"

"Fuck you."

"Rudy!" said his mother, "There is no reason to be rude."

Miriam, Levi, and Mary were sunning on a rock in the middle of the river when Levi heard the first dull and distant whap-whap of the approaching helicopters.

"Something's coming," he said.

Miriam was immediately alert. She had come to trust Levi's hearing much more than her own.

"What is it?" asked Mary, sensing that Miriam was very tense.

"I don't know, but it's coming this way."

"Quick!" ordered Miriam getting off the rock and heading toward the cave.

"I have to go back," said Mary.

"Come with us. It will be safer. It might be Germans."

"No. I have to find my mom. It's probably nothing. I'll see you back at the cabin," she said, and ran to the path on the other side of the river.

The helicopters had become loud enough for Miriam to hear. "Hurry!" she said, and they ran to hide.

One of the helicopters came in low; its rotor wash bent the treetops with fury. A concussion grenade landed in the middle of the yard and exploded. Everyone was knocked to the ground. Six uniformed Orpo agents followed right behind it and quickly bound the wrists and ankles of the dazed group. Mary came running into the yard, "Mother!" she screamed and threw herself down next to her.

The other helicopter hovered overhead watching for anyone they might have missed.

Quickly and without discussion, Miriam and Levi grabbed their bags and packs and hurried away. They had planned their escape routes and had practiced stealing away often enough that they knew just what to do. They were far away and still moving before the Orpo began searching for them.

Rick Bogle

Afterword

Unfortunately, "Tell Me Your Story" isn't as fictional as it may appear. The historical setting is fictional as are the names of the characters. And, also obviously, breeding humans for use in research isn't legal. But humans aren't the only animals on earth who experience profound suffering, profound joy, love, humor, inventiveness, curiosity, bravery, deceit, or any other characteristic we might ascribe moral or ethical import to. Humans aren't the only animals who are psychologically crushed by isolation, deprivation, or torture. The scientific literature is replete with reams of published papers reporting on the results of experiments demonstrating the close cognitive characteristics of humans and many other animals. As sure as the brutality of the labs in "Tell Me Your Story" wounded Miriam and Levi, so too does the brutality in the animal labs today hurt the monkeys, dogs, cats, rabbits, rats, mice, and all the other animals who suffer unseen and unheard.

Just as the details of the experiments occurring in the labs in the story were kept secret, the details of experiments occurring in the animal labs today are just as guarded. In 2009, when the CIA destroyed 92 videotapes of the interrogations it conducted on people they suspected of being associated with Al-Qaeda, many observers recognized that they were likely destroying clear evidence of the United States Government torturing people. In 2006, the University of Wisconsin, Madison destroyed 628 videotapes of experiments on monkeys after four years of fighting to keep them out of activists' hands. Multiple public records requests were repeatedly denied because the university feared the backlash if the public could see what actually goes on in the labs.

But just as a little information from the labs in the story trickled out into the public arena, a little information trickles out of the animal labs. For instance, in the monkey labs, the cages really do have squeeze backs. Resistance really is futile.

Estimates of the number of people killed by the 1918 Spanish flu range from between 20 and 100 million people. It was extinct; researchers actually did dig up victims' bodies in the Canadian permafrost and resurrect the most deadly disease ever encountered. Now, they are infecting animals with the disease—mice, ferrets, and monkeys—and recording the details of their lungs filling with bloody mucus as they die.

In the fictitious Hamm and Kals experiment, the scientists breed highly anxious Jews so that they can frighten them and then dissect their brains.

105

Tell Me Your Story

This is now being done with monkeys at the University of Wisconsin, Madison. In the mid-1990s, researchers Ned Kalin, Steve Shelton, and Richard Davidson learned to identify monkeys with "trait-like anxious behavior." Over the years, they burned out parts of young fearful monkeys' brains with acid, frightened them, and then killed them. Today, scientists in university laboratories across the county are still using experimental brain lesions to study fear in monkeys and other animals.

The people doing these things deny that they are hurting the animals, much like Dr. Gottlieb's denial during the debate that the scientists were being cruel. In 2009, I was on a television news panel with Richard Davidson. He was adamant that the monkeys undergoing the brain surgeries, being frightened, and killed, weren't being hurt.

Archie Nelson recalls the experiments in which women who are pregnant with female fetuses are injected with testosterone. This too is being done to monkeys at the University of Wisconsin. They have learned that large enough doses at the right time result in female monkeys being born with grossly deformed genitals and seriously impaired endocrine systems.

When Miriam talks about chewing on her arms, this isn't a fabrication either. Peer reviewed research has shown clearly that most monkeys in the labs have abnormal behaviors and sometimes bite and wound themselves. In severe cases, they can chew off their own fingers and the ends of their tails. Life in the labs is crushingly oppressive.

The brutality depicted in the "subhuman" labs is also common in the animal labs. Every time an undercover investigator is able to infiltrate a lab, the videos they bring out show animals being punched, screamed at, and manhandled.

And what about Schimmelpfennig's challenge near the end of the story? Were Miriam and Levi really better off in the lab where they could be taken care of properly? Every time animal right activists liberate animals from labs or from farms, that's exactly what the industry claims.

And if cures and breakthroughs were being made because of the experiments, did the benefits outweigh the costs?

If you thought Archie, Cindy, and Rudy were the heroes, and Miriam and Levi, and the other Jews were victims, and the Germans were the villains, then you may have terrorist tendencies, because you must think that there are times that legality matters much less than morality. That thought is dangerous to government. You should turn yourself in right now, or, maybe you should learn the details of what's going on in the labs in your own neighborhood.

Is it unfair to compare these two scenarios, one fictitious and the other factual? Is it unfair to Jewish people, or does it suggest that Jews are no better than monkeys?

I don't think it is unfair to Jews, and I don't think Jews are better than dogs either; I don't think you, whoever you are, Jew, gentile, or heathen, are better than a monkey, a dog, or a cow. All suffering is of a like kind. It is the suffering that matters, not who is suffering.

There is a wealth of scientific evidence that animals other than humans have emotions, desires, preferences, ideas, that they love, laugh, and experience the world in ways much like we do. It is these similarities that matter, not differences in raw intelligence and definitely not differences in power.

We have power over all other species, just like the Nazi's in the story had power over all other races. The Nazi's chose to view themselves as the Master Race, superior, deserving, and always right. But this is exactly how we see ourselves when it comes to our relationship with other animals. It is grotesque and monstrous bigotry in both cases.

Rick Bogle
Madison, Wisconsin
(Revised, 2017)

The Risks of Empathy

Chapter 1

Bob stepped off the curb into the small puddle of brown water which distracted him just long enough for the bus to run him over. A police officer sitting in a parked cruiser saw the accident and made an immediate call for an ambulance. The bus driver made a similar call only an instant later. Two ambulances arrived, surprisingly fast. Two paramedic teams were quickly at Bob's side and saved his life. Bob had every reason to expect to live another eighty or ninety years, at least; he was only a hundred and forty-two years old after all.

Sarah drove up to her front door wondering what to make for dinner that night. After a little thought she decided on fried chicken. Jimmy and Amanda both loved it and Dave always said that her fried chicken is the best he'd ever had. Fried chicken always made her think of her mom. "Sarah," she would say, "remember to always peal the skin from the chicken and fry it in low fat canola." That always made Sarah smile. Thinking of Jimmy and Amanda, she tried to imagine what it must have been like for parents back in her mom's and grandmother's times who knew their children were going to die and needed to be protected even from things like cholesterol, salmonella, or cancer.

108

The damn thing just wouldn't work. Stan and Earnie were sitting on backless swivel stools facing each other. Earnie had a pair of blue virtual vision goggles on and was wearing something that looked like a hairnet. Stan had a sensor in his hand and was moving it from intersection to intersection while watching the readout on the sensor and occasionally glancing over at two video displays that appeared to be showing two rapidly undulating graphs.

"I don't know what the fuck's wrong with the damn thing," Earnie said from behind the goggles.

"We're gonna get it," answered Stan reassuringly.

And then Earnie seemed to relax and said, "Oh, god."

Karen was finally going to graduate and was going to make her first career choice. Her grades had been excellent and all her professors had written her glowing recommendations. She had met with the councilors and they had given her all the brochures to read; but even without them she knew what career she was going to choose. Without more than a second glance at the code for Conservationist, she coded the appropriate boxes and became the country's newest Basic Biological Research Scientist Trainee for about two and a half minutes until some equally bright and dynamic young scholar took her place as the nation's newest scientist.

In 2021, Dr. Robert N. Diggins discovered that a particularly long series of nucleotides in human cells seemed to be misplaced. Using gene-splicing techniques that had been in use for decades, Diggins rearranged things. The order had only been a little off according to Diggins's research. Ten years later scientists generally recognized Diggins as a total crackpot, but a damned lucky one. Based on erroneous data and faulty reasoning, Diggins had discovered the fountain of youth and the Diggins Adjustment had become something akin to circumcision. It had taken eight years for the public to force the government to act, but now, with the gene rearrangement, humans had become immune to essentially all disease. Rumors continued to pop up for years about this or that rare disease, but now everyone generally agreed that they just might not die.

The Risks of Empathy

Bob got out of the hospital fairly easily after his run in with the bus. His liver had been damaged quite badly, but techniques had come a long way from his grandfather's time. Bob's liver had been removed and placed in a nutrient bath and allowed to rest and heal more quickly. While Bob's liver was getting its healing rest, Bob stayed attached to the artificial liver and watched videos. An artificial lens had been placed in his right eye, which had been punctured in the accident, but now he had excellent vision in that eye. When Bob left the hospital his liver was rested and his vision, in one eye at least, was sharp.

Feeling really old fashioned, Sarah took the chicken from the freezer. How many people still stored their meat in the freezer? An entire craze had embraced meat that was beginning to decompose and soften. Sarah did keep some meat in the cabinet but she found that the ventilating fan didn't completely removed the rotting meat's bad odor. The chicken thawed out in an instant in the microwave. Sarah liked to cook. She put the black cast iron pan on the electric burner and spooned in three cups of the best snow-white pork lard. She went to the refrigerator, thinking of being old fashioned again, took out half a dozen eggs and cracked them into a bowl. To this she added a cup of heavy cream. She took the cracker crumbs from the shelf and dumped them into a flat blue dish and sprinkled in some salt and pepper. She cut the chicken into her natural parts: legs, wings, breast, thighs, and back and set the giblets and neck aside. She dipped a piece of the chicken into the egg and heavy cream, then into the crumbs, then back into the egg and cream and crumbs once more and then into the almost smoking hot fat. The skin sizzled as she repeated the process with another and another piece until the pan was full. She went back and turned each piece while the aroma of frying chicken filled the house.

"It was fucking beyond real, man," said Earnie. He looked down at the foam in his coffee mug and watched the colors change from reds and greens to blues as the oil slid off the bubbles. "It was fucking beyond real, man."

Stan knew they were going to be very wealthy. Their research into virtual reality had hit pay dirt. When he had switched places with Earnie, he understood Earnie's rapture. Their cerebral transmitter had achieved a step, a light-year's leap past the virt-vision in use. This was so real that someone might get hurt reacting from the images in their mind and before their eyes.

Karen began her new career at the Enzyme Interaction Institute in Dr. Yu's laboratory. Yu's people were working to learn whether the ratio of neurons to muscle fibers in hamster thigh muscle was quantitatively different than the n/m ratio in guinea pig thigh muscle. The first of the many responsibilities Karen was eventually assigned was the care of the experimental animals in building number seven. Karen would begin cleaning at nine in the morning. The hamsters and guinea pigs were stored in clear plastic tubs with light blue snap-on plastic lids. A water bottle was attached to one end, a simple food tray was attached at the other. Karen pushed a cart as she walked down the rows of cages. There were two tall stacks of the clear plastic tubs stacked like Dixie cups on the cart. Next to the tubs was a five-gallon bucket of food pellets. A pistol grip hose nozzle was hooked over the edge of the cart which pulled a black water hose along behind it. Karen stopped at the first bank of tubs. The stainless steel rack was twelve tubs wide and five tubs high. She cleaned a half rack at a time. These were guinea pig tubs; the hamster tubs were twenty-four tubs wide and ten tubs high. Each aisle was made up of twenty banks of racks. All the tubs along the first five aisles held experimental animals. Each of these tubs held one animal. The other three aisles held pregnant mothers or mothers and babies.

The Diggins Adjustment, or simply the Adjustment as it came to be known, was a boon to food producers and tobacco growers and chemical corporations and turned life insurance companies into holders of vast amounts of money. People quit dying, but it was a decade or two before people really began to understand and canceled their life insurance. The food producers quit caring about the health benefits of their products, and low fat options disappeared overnight. Tobacco became immensely popular once again and though a few restaurants still tried to maintain a no-smoking area, the notion was considered quaint more than anything else. Chemical companies quit worrying about carcinogenicity and pollution and went into free-for-all production.

The world experienced a renaissance - no illness, no death, nothing but potential.

Chapter 2

Harry Mahoney massaged his temples with his right hand and held a paper cup of stale coffee in his left. He felt old, and well he should have, for although he looked like he was about fifty, Harry was ninety-six years old. He had been called out this evening and taken away from a nice dream about kids and the lake he and his parents had visited many years ago. But now he stood at the base of the old McGreggor Building at the corner of Main and 2nd. There didn't seem to be much left of the jumper. The twenty-two-story drop had splashed her for half a block. The roads were slick from the oily wet mist that seemed to hang over the city these days; a trickle of water ran down the back of Harry's neck.

"Why the hell do they even call us for jumpers anymore?" he asked to no one in particular. The paramedic with the squeegee looked at him and shrugged. Harry signed something for the medic and turned and walked away, tossing the mostly empty coffee cup into the gutter along with the rest of the garbage. He had seen four jumpers this week.

Harry looked up at a clock on a building: a little after three. No point in going back to bed; by the time he got home it would almost be time to get up. Harry glanced up and down the street and saw the flickering neon sign: *Jim's Lounge.*

Walking through the door Harry stepped into a small dark smoky bar with the odor of old plastic, old beer, and old urine combining to create a comfortable womb-like haven. Harry settled into a booth and noticed through the haze that half a dozen other people were seated around the room. The bartender came over and tossed down a coaster and took Harry's order for an Old Crow highball. What the hell, the day was going to be a long one anyway.

A woman walked up and sat down across from Harry.

"Startin' early aren't ya?" she inquired.

Harry looked at her with the practiced eye of seventy years as a detective. She was small and had a dark mustache that belied her blond wig. Her nails were painted a dark blue that failed to hide the dirt under her nails. She smiled at Harry and revealed teeth that had not been brushed in a very long time.

Rick Bogle

"Buy a girl a drink?"

Harry motioned for the barkeep and she ordered a Pink Lady.

"Name's Rita. I haven't seen you in here before." Rita looked at Harry with veiled interest.

"No, I was on the way home. It's been a long night. I was called to investigate the jumper down the street. Maybe you heard the sirens."

"Yeah, I heard them. You a cop or something?"

"Detective Mahoney. Call me Harry."

"Was it a man or a woman?" asked Rita. "I got a theory that it's mostly women jumpin'."

"A woman; what's your theory?"

"Well Harry, it goes something like this: You might not believe it to look at me, and I know it ain't polite to say, but I'm a hundred and ten fucking years old and I'm damn tired."

Harry knew what she was getting at and nodded; he was tired too.

"Well, what's the fuckin' point anyway? If I live to be two hundred god-damned years old, I mean what's the fuckin' point? See, I think women get it better than men. Men always think that if they just try hard enough, or maybe get the right fuckin' breaks that they can fix any god-damned problem that comes up."

"Maybe you could find something interesting to take up your time," began Harry, but Rita cut him off.

"That's what I'm fuckin' talkin' about. I tell you about a problem and you think you got the answer, but you're full of shit."

Harry was beginning to realize that Rita had been drinking long before he came in. Alcoholism didn't really matter any more; you couldn't tell people they were hurting themselves – sclerosis was one of those ancient concerns like cancer or AIDS. He couldn't even suggest that she see a priest; churches had disappeared as new bars opened. It seemed people didn't really care too much about salvation any more in a world where death and disease had been essentially beaten.

Harry stood up and laid a fin on the dark oily tabletop. "Have another on me," he said as he put his hat back on and headed towards the door.

"Right," Rita said as he stepped out the door, "like you got somewhere to go and something to do that matters."

113

Chapter 3

Karen was more excited than she had been in weeks. She had cleaned more hamster and guinea pig cages than she had imagined even existed. That morning, on the magnetic white duty board, she had seen her name stuck in a new location: Dr. Yu's assistant.

In the laboratory she prepared everything just as she had been taught at the university. She had the gleaming sterile instruments all prepared on the pale green plastic tray and the four tubs of research animals: two hamsters and two guinea pigs, on the cart next to the laboratory table.

Dr. Yu came in wearing a crisply starched white lab coat and latex gloves. His dark hair was combed straight back and seemed covered in some sort of grease. He seemed momentarily surprised by Karen's presence. She thought he must have forgotten that she had been assigned to assist him, or maybe he had not been told. Yu mumbled something, looked around at Karen's preparations and seemed satisfied. He turned his attention to the tubs and chose one of the small ones first. Yu popped the blue top off and reached in with one motion. Karen was startled at how quickly he broke the hamster's neck. Almost before it had quit quivering Yu had cut out a small portion of its thigh and placed it into one of the vials Karen had standing by. In less than five minutes Yu had performed the same procedure on the other hamster and the two guinea pigs.

Karen loved science.

A little over a year after their breakthrough, Stan and Earnie's cerebral transmitter had evolved and been repackaged by the global marketing giant Selling Inc. Selling's production team had learned that the experiences one had when "plugged in" seemed absolutely real. Volunteers who had watched downhill skiing recordings had broken legs and arms when the person skiing and recording their experience had fallen.

Harry sat on the edge of his bed with his head in his hands. He noticed the darkly stained sheet covering the sagging mattress and wondered idly to himself how long it had been since he had put fresh linen on the bed. Years he figured.

"Happy fuckin' birthday," he thought to himself. He had turned ninety-eight last night, and as far as he could tell he was going to be around for a very long time. The thought of the endless days of work ahead encouraged him to pick up the can on the bedside table and down the stale dregs of last night's last beer. Harry rose from the bed, walked over to the window and looked out on the gray sky, gray skyline, and gray skyscrapers blocking his view of endlessly more gray buildings. He put his hand down the front of his stained Jockey's and absently held his penis and testicles. It was Tuesday at 11:00 AM. It was his regular day off. He wondered what he would do to kill the day and walked over to the purring refrigerator for a fresh cold one. And, as luck would have it, there was only one left. Harry popped the tab and downed it in a single gulp. Oh well, the trip to the store would get him out of the apartment.

Dr. Robert sat across from the couple and tried to guess their ages, though he realized it was an impossible task in this day and age. But she appeared to be mid-thirties maybe and him just a little older.

"How old are you two?" An impolite question in recent years but one a doctor could still get away with.

"Sharon's one forty something doc, and I'm pushing two hundred. How old are you?" the man asked, tit for tat.

"Well, I don't know if that's…"

"Look, you asked us, so what's fair's fair," the man snapped back.

Dr. Robert sat for a moment, "I'm one fifty-two."

"OK then, you can see what we're sayin'. We don't want our kid to get Adjusted. We want to have her at home and let her get to grow old and die."

"You know that's illegal? I could lose my license if someone found out and reported me. I'm supposed to report you just for asking, you know."

"Look doc, we came here because someone said you were a good guy and could be trusted. If we got it wrong you can just say we never came in." The man took his hand off his wife's still shapely stomach and said, "Let's get out of here Sharon."

"No, wait, I'll help you. I just have to be so careful. I hope you can understand."

The man settled back down and seemed to shed a few years from his countenance.

"Let's get you on the table for an exam, Sharon."

The Risks of Empathy

Richard Selling sat across the gleaming walnut conference table from the Secretary of Commerce and wondered to himself just what the feds were actually willing to pay.

"As I mentioned earlier Mr. Selling, our top experts feel that if more people had access to your Total Experience device that there would be far fewer jumpers and 'accidental' car and train accidents." He leaned heavily on 'accidental'.

"How many is 'more' Mr. Secretary? We are in full production now and can barely keep them on the shelves."

"Yes, well, we think, um, well, everyone should have one."

"We think so too Mr. Secretary, and we are hoping to increase production by opening a new plant next year." He could see from the Secretary's expression that he might have missed the point. "Did you mean, literally, everyone?"

"Well, um, well, say everyone over fifty?"

Selling did some quick mental math. "Mr. Secretary we don't have that sort of production capability at the moment..."

"No, no, you misunderstand our proposition. You see, we do have the resources. We want to, well, um, yes, license the product and would be willing to pay some fair amount per unit. We, um, well, I have been authorized to offer you, say, one hundred dollars per unit," he lied.

"We are selling them now for two thousand a pop, why would we...?"

"I'm sorry for not making our position a bit more clear. We are talking about a, well, um, yes, well, a lump sum payment."

"A lump sum payment?" More mental math. "But people turn fifty every day and you said..."

"Yes, well, um, we, uh, our experts tell us that we can expect eight hundred million people to be over the age of fifty within the next ten years. So, um, well, er, how does eighty billion dollars sound? Does that seem fair? We really have to do something about all the suicides we think. Our experts tell us that the strains on the system will be just too great if ..." he shut up quickly, realizing that had rambled on in exactly the way he had wished to avoid.

Selling sat enthralled. The government had just offered to cut him an eighty billion dollar check. "My god," he thought to himself, "they must really think there is a real problem. He had known that the feds had been keeping the number of suicides under-reported, but this suggested that they were keeping them seriously hushed up. He knew he had them.

"Make it one hundred even and you've got yourself a deal, Mr. Secretary."

"You are a true patriot Mr. Selling. The country owes you a real debt of gratitude." He was secretly quite pleased with himself; he had been authorized to go to one thousand each.

Chapter 4

Sarah had prepared a lovely dinner of full-fatted pork loins with her special bacon and cream gravy. The dessert, the richest chocolate mousse made with the thickest cream available, was chilling in the refrigerator.

"Honey! It's time to eat! Tell the kids to put their videos away now."

Sarah's husband stepped into the dining room with the cigar smoke following him into the room like a cloud of exhaust follows a semi. "Ah Sarah, do we have to eat at the table? It is Saturday, and the kids are really having fun with their new TEs. Heck, I'm havin' fun too. Can't we just eat and play with the TEs at the same time?"

Sarah looked at the set table and realized that she probably was going to have to give in.

"Well, but you have to promise that we can eat like a real family tomorrow then. I want to make the veal and lard patties that I saw on that cooking show yesterday."

"Sure Honey, it is Saturday after all."

Rita stepped into the hall of her apartment building and didn't notice the old urine smell and the shouts coming from this and that apartment. So many years of living in a rundown hellhole had dulled her sensory organs to the din and olfactory assaults. She made it to the ninth floor and unlocked the graffiti covered door to number 908. The number was not really discernible any longer, but it didn't matter because she never had guests who might need to find the apartment number anyway. She stepped though the doorway and quickly locked the three dead bolts and latched the three security chains. That done, she relaxed imperceptibly and walked into the kitchen of her small efficiency which was really little more than a sink, hot plate, and small refrigerator.

Cold beer in hand, Rita made her way over to the very worn and stained recliner that might have once been red, but was now decidedly worn brick, and settled into the seat that conformed perfectly to her after three decades of breaking in. She looked at the TE sitting on her coffee table and wondered for the thousandth time, just what the government was up to by giving these things away. The brief directions that had come with the damn thing had explained that the battery in it was good for at least a year and could be replaced free of charge at any U.S. Post Office. Free! Humph! Rita had never seen anything free in her very long life and wasn't about to start believing in fairies quite yet.

Down at the bar, it seemed like the damn things were all that anyone was talking about. "Did you get yours?" "Have you tried it out?" "Did you try the skiing program? Or the Paris trip? Or the sex show?" It was all anyone could talk about alright, but, noticed Rita, they were all still alive, hell, maybe even a little more alive that she could remember them being in a goodly long time. They didn't seem to be getting sick or acting like zombies or anything....

The TE worked simply enough. Selling Inc. engineers had refined the original version so that now all there was to it was a very light hairnet. No wires attached the net to the black plastic control box, which was itself about the size of a pack of cigarettes. There was an LED tuner that worked just like a radio tuner. "Channels" or "programs" as Rita had learned from the barroom chatter were transmitted exactly like radio. Only instead of listening to a song, you now experienced something that seemed real. Rita was still suspicious, but she was also very bored. She put the net on her head, and with more than just a little apprehension, she pressed the power button.

An attractive man in a dark sweater and light slacks was suddenly standing about five feet away from Rita. He had his hands up, palms outward in the universal "I mean you no harm" gesture.

"Don't be alarmed. I'm not real. If at any time you get nervous simply press the power butto.."

And he was gone. Just like that. Rita had almost peed when the man appeared and was shaken by how real he had seemed. She pressed the power button again.

The attractive man appeared exactly as he had first appeared. He had his hands up, palms outward in the universal "I mean you no harm" gesture.

"Don't be alarmed. I'm not real. If at any time you get nervous simply press the power button and the Total Experience will stop immediately. This is an introduction to the Selling Total Experience, if at any time you would like to skip this introduction simply tune to a new channel. The tuner automatically starts at the beginning of a program, so you will always be able to have a Total Experience."

He blathered on and on and Rita soon found herself getting a little bored with his prattle, in spite of the novelty of him seeming to actually be in the room with her and his good looks. Then, something caught her attention.

"The Total Experience is not like watching a movie or high definition TV. If it were what you are seeing now might be as much as you could expect. When you tune to the Total Experience experiences you will feel as if you are experiencing an actual event. Remember, this is not real and you can always turn off the power. We recommend that you use the Selling Total Experience only when seated in a comfortable and preferably soft chair or from the safety of your bed. Selling Inc. will not be held liable due to accidents associated with this devise under special agreement with the United States government. Happy Experiencing!

The attractive man appeared exactly as he had first appeared. He had his hands up, palms outward in the universal "I mean you no harm" gesture. "Don't be alarmed. I'm not real. If at any time you get nervous simply press the power button and the Total Experience will stop immediately. This is an introduction to the Selling Total Experience, if at any time you would like to…"

And he was gone again the instant Rita shut the thing off.

Chapter 5

Working in Yu's laboratory promised to many doors for Karen. Yu's prestige attracted some of the top biomedical scientists to the Enzyme Interaction Institute and they all came occasionally to Yu for advice. Karen was able to tag along as Dr. Yu toured the various labs, and she learned much about the experiments taking place at Enzyme.

In one lab they were trying to transplant dog kidneys into baboons, and in another, they were trying to transplant baboon kidneys into dogs. Years ago, Karen knew, massive investigation had gone into trying to transplant pig organs into monkeys and that those experiments had always been disastrous failures. She had always imagined that the Diggins Adjustment had ended xeno-transplantation experiments.

In another lab, scientists were using cats to study the way heroin slowed a cat's iris's reaction to sudden bright light. In anther lab, mice were being bred with novel genetic deformities and their abilities to navigate mazes to find food and avoid electro-shock documented and analyzed.

The Risks of Empathy

Once, while assisting Dr. Yu kill guinea pigs, Karen had unthinkingly asked, "Dr. Yu? Why are we studying dog and baboon kidney transplants now? My uncle injured a kidney in a football accident when he was in high school, and they just cloned a new one for him from his own kidney."

Karen was startled by Yu's abrupt response. "Science does not have to have a reason! We study! We Learn! We are scientists!"

Karen had never seen the usually quiet researcher react so spontaneously. She recognized that she had struck a sensitive nerve and was thankful she had not asked why his lab was comparing the ratio of neurons to muscle fibers in hamster and guinea pig thigh muscles. Karen thought Yu was even quieter and more distant during the following few days.

Rita was falling at about 120 mph at almost two miles above the earth. The wind against her felt like water and she could move through it like she was body surfing in Hawaiian waves. It was as if she could see forever—even the curvature of the earth was discernable. At twelve hundred feet she pulled the ripcord and the red and blue paraglider inflated behind her slowing her descent as she soared silently over the Grand Canyon and peered down at the rapids and an occasional group of deer.

She glided gracefully in and landed with barely a stumble.

The man in the dark sweater appeared again and said, "If you would like to paraglide over the Grand Canyon again, press replay."

It was the sweetheart deal of all time. Richard Selling had pocketed a cool $100 billion and had acquired the contract for broadcasting the TEs. He had immediately sent people all over the world with the experience recorders and was producing ten to twenty new experiences a month for broadcast. His deal with the government gave him a commission for each new experience Selling Inc. made available. They didn't seem to care what it was. Because it was virtual, once recorded, no one felt much moral compunction about the experiences they were having. There seemed though, to be high demand for them all, whether sexual, athletic, or even culinary. There was even a demand for entirely cerebral experiences. One of Selling's agents had gotten the idea to have a mathematician record the experience of solving an especially complex equation. The thrill and understanding of the beauty of the math had never been accessible to

120

the general public. But now, people, albeit a relatively small portion of the entire experiencing public, were actually able to understand and feel what a deep insight into mathematics was actually like. Selling himself found these inner mental and emotional experiences to be quite moving.

An especially popular series was "Falling in Love." Young adults had been asked to wear the recorders for a period of months. The payoff had come when a few had become infatuated with someone else. The experience of falling in love seemed to be as popular as any that Selling was offering and they continually got requests for more of the series.

Chapter 6

Harry sat in his car reading the paper. The street was damp; a sheen of oil covered everything. The air was typically heavy with smog; the sun was a dull spot just visible between a row of tall gray concrete skyscrapers. Across the street a man sat in a doorway; he seemed to be dozing. Few people came and went into the building, probably because it was the middle of the day and most people were either working or plugged into their TEs.

Harry noticed a small article in the business section about the decline in suicides in the city. He had noticed that there seemed to be fewer jumpers than usual. The article suggested that suicide rates had always risen and fallen throughout history. Harry figured it had something to do with the fact that people were not quite as bored as they had been. Even he had found the new TEs to be alluring and time consuming. And consuming time was an important consideration these days.

A man in a black sweatshirt and a young girl, who to Harry's practiced eye seemed to be resisting the arm around her shoulders, walked up the steps and spoke briefly to the man in the doorway. The three of them went into the building.

Harry radioed the station that he required back up, gave the building address, got quickly out of the car and followed them into the dark building. The elevator was out of order, of course, and Harry could hear them walking in the stairwell. He followed quietly and made sure he kept against the wall so as not to be seen from above.

They pushed open the door and left the stairs on the fourth floor. Harry hurried to catch up and just as he made it to the door and looked out, he saw a door close down the dank hallway. Harry quickly and very quietly hurried to the room, put his ear against the dented graffiti-covered door and listened for a moment. Satisfied, he hurried back to the stairs and radioed once again with the floor and room number.

Satisfied that help was on the way, Harry was quickly back in place outside the room and listening through the door. He heard a sound from the girl that suggested he didn't have much time to waste. Without hesitation, and with many years of practice, Harry pulled his pistol and made short work of the doorjamb and doorknob. He pushed his way through the door and was greeted by the surprised faces of the two men. One reached for his own gun and Harry shot him in the head. The other man was wearing an experience recorder and was seated in a chair next to the table where the girl was tied down and also wearing a recorder. The second man had the good sense not to move.

Suddenly, they were joined by four uniformed officers. One of them was handcuffing the man wearing the recorder, another was helping the young girl who was obviously in shock and another knelt beside the man with the hole through his head.

"Not much hope for this guy."

"Nope," answered Harry. "Modern medicine still can't rebuild a brain demolished by a 45 at close range. That's too bad."

"Looks like a torture-murder gig," one of the officers said.

On the table next to the girl was a pair of pliers, a razor, a bottle of alcohol, and a cigarette lighter.

"Yep. We've been watching this guy for some time. We've confiscated some of the TEs he's been black-marketing."

"These people are really sick."

"Yep. Last month we found eight different illegal TEs. Rapes, murders, torture executions, really horrible things being sold in a dozen different locations. It seems to be a growing fad. Get this scum down to the station, and take the girl to County Med. I'll initial your reports when I get back to the station. Make sure no one messes with the recorders."

"Got it."

Stan and Earnie had reaped a handsome sum from their invention of the cerebral transmitter that was now so widely known as the Selling Total Experience. They had taken the money and retired for a while to a Mexican beach. Though lovely and warm, it wasn't long before the lush tropical luxury began to tire them both. They had always been most excited by discovery and invention. Without much discussion, they pooled their resources and bought a new laboratory replete with the best electronics money could buy.

Back to work, they had decided to pursue their original investigations into the transmission of thoughts and perceptions. They decided to see whether they could look into the mind of another species.

Ted was Stan's large mixed breed dog. He seemed to have some shepherd and collie ancestry, but there seemed to be some hound in the woodpile as well. He was dark, had long ears, longish hair, and was always with Stan. Earnie joked occasionally that if Stan had to choose between him and Ted, that Ted would win out. Stan never contradicted Earnie's claim.

Ted was good-natured and seemed not to mind the hat Stan was having him wear every now and then. The hat was, of course, an experience recorder modified to fit the dog.

Stan sat with a net on his own head while both he and Earnie worked at their own computer consoles.

"Look at the spikes in Ted's alpha and epsilon waves," said Stan. "I think we have to modify the input to coincide with the third band in the recorder."

"Right," answered Earnie, and he modified an algorithm in the program. "What are you getting?"

"Not too much. Something."

"Maybe Ted's just not too aware of his environment," joked Earnie. "Hum. How 'bout this?' And he fiddled with another parameter. "What now?"

"What now?" he repeated. "Hey Stan! Are you getting anything more?"

Earnie looked up from his computer and over at his friend. Stan seemed to be having some sort of mild seizure. His eyes seemed unfocused and his shoulders were twitching slightly. A bit of drool ran from the corner of his mouth. The slight smile on his face kept Earnie from pulling the plug on Stan's head net. He sat twitching and drooling for maybe five minutes while Earnie watched the computer monitors in fascination.

Finally, Stan moved his hand slowly to the computer keyboard and stopped the experiment himself. He went over and sat down next to the large dog and put his arms around his neck and began to make a noise that seemed to Earnie to be a mix of a quiet laugh and a shaking sob.

Chapter 7

On October 16, 2159, after much discussion and heated debate, Selling Inc. began broadcasting a new series of Total Experiences. In all, there were ten Experiences in the set.

Rita had become something of a TE junky. She was spending much less time at the bar these days and figured that to be a good thing, if only for the savings. Now she simply drank alone at home with the TE. She had experienced all the "Falling in Love" series many times each. She learned that she liked surfing and skydiving. She had tried a couple of the sex experiences, but she could take them or leave them. She figured it must be her age.

Every time a new Experience was announced, Rita was quick to give it a go. She had come to think of herself as adventuresome. Of course, her adventures all took place in her gray apartment from her worn recliner, but no matter, when she had her TE turned on, she was someone else, somewhere wonderful.

She was a cow. By her side was the most perfect creature in the world, her calf. Licking him was heaven. He smelled like nothing she had smelled before, and she simply could not get enough of his sweet aroma into her cool wet nostrils. She looked up and around her and all she could see were other cows with their own calves and green grass and blue sky and she felt the deepest contentment she had ever known.

A sound grew in her ear. Looking over her shoulder she saw a thing that made her quiver with fear. The thing had others with it. She could think only of her calf. She bellowed loudly to tell the other cows and moved to be between the things and her baby.

Soon they were all around her and the other cows, pushing and yelling. She was afraid and could hear the fear in her calf as he began crying loudly. Soon all the calves and cows were yelling and the fear was everywhere. They hurried this way and that trying to keep the new calves from being accidentally stepped on and then they were all trapped.

They put something on her calf's neck and pulled him away. Her anger was strong and she tried to protect him, but they hurt her and were much stronger. She could hear him crying and she kept calling to him. Her pain and worry and fear and bravery were overwhelming.

The man in the dark sweater appeared and said, "If you would like to experience being a cow again, press replay."

Rita pressed the stop button. She was back, alone in her gray apartment.

She remembered that she had a quarter pound of ground round in the cabinet over the hot plate and, shaking, she vomited the entire contents of her stomach.

Sarah called Dave and the kids, Jimmy and Amanda, to dinner.

As everyone took their place at the table, Sarah asked Jimmy, "How was school today sweetheart?"

"What's that?" said Amanda as she sat down at her place across from Jimmy.

"That's your mom's famous stuffed pork chops, young lady," answered her father. I seem to remember you eating two of them last time we had 'em. Eh Jimmy?"

Dave looked over at his son who seemed to be almost as white as the tablecloth.

"What's wrong, Jim?"

"Where do you get pork chops?" asked Amanda.

"Well, honey," said her mom, "I get them down at Republix market. The butcher always cuts them extra thick for me. You remember Mr. Johnson. I think you were there with me last week when I bought them. Why sure you were. Don't you remember?"

"I know where you bought them, mom. Where do pork chops come from, though?"

"Oh!" chuckled Dave. "You mean what part of the pig are the chops. They're kind of near the ribs, aren't they Sarah?"

At this both Jimmy and Amanda stood up and began shouting almost at once about how horrible it was that they had killed a pig and didn't they know how scared the pig was and how could they do this and then they both ran into Amanda's room and Dave and Sarah could hear them still yelling and crying and simply carrying on.

"Now what do you suppose has gotten in to them?" said Dave looking with confusion toward his wife.

Chapter 8

Richard Selling, president, CEO and founder of the mega-giant marketing conglomerate, Selling Inc. was not used to being summoned.

The Risks of Empathy

Nevertheless, when the president called personally and asked him to stop by for a chat, Selling didn't give the thought of saying "no thanks" much consideration. He had a good idea what the meeting was about.

Selling sat at a conference table with President John Adams, the secretary of state, and the attorney general. The attorney general had a single thin manila folder in front of him. Everyone else was provided with a glass of water. A crystal pitcher of water had been provided for each of the participants.

Secretary of State, Rebecca McGuire, a woman of stature and brilliance, was leading the discussion.

"Mr. Selling, we invited you here as a courtesy based on your prior service to your country. We thought it best to have a face-to-face and frank discussion regarding the criminal charges we are going to file against Selling Inc. today."

"Just hold on Rebecca," began the president. We haven't actually decided to go ahead with the criminal charges have we? Sam?"

Attorney General, Samuel B. Wilkins, reputed to be the best trial lawyer and legal mind of the decade, and rumored to have higher aspirations, did not even glance at the president. His eyes remained steadfast on his prey.

"What's going on here?" began Selling. "You people are outside the law. Why wasn't I told to bring legal counsel? This is outrageous!"

Wilkins withdrew a single sheet of White House stationary from the manila folder. "Mr. Selling, this document grants you complete immunity concerning the government's case against Selling Inc. At this point in time, you need no counsel."

The secretary of state picked up the conversation. "Mr. Selling, we recognize that you could not have known the far-reaching effects that the recent release of the animal TEs were going to have on the nation's, the global, economy. But the past two weeks, as you are aware, have been unprecedented in human history. The loss to the U.S. economy is likely to be in the trillions of dollars and we are hearing rumors of outbreaks of violence across the country and from around the world."

"Violence?" said Selling. "I haven't heard anything about much violence."

"We have been successful in our attempt to keep it contained. I'm sure a man of your experience can recognize the dangers to our society should certain unscrupulous types hear that unrest and armed conflict are occurring."

"Just what is happening?"

McGuire looked over at Wilkins and the president.

Adams stood up and said, "Damn it to hell Wilkins! If we don't bring him in who the hell else do we have?"

"Alright John, but you know my concern."

The president walked over to an antique sideboard that had been a gift to the White House from the French people back when there was a France, and the White House was still in need of furniture. He pressed a discretely placed button under the table's edge. "Jenny," he said. "Give us the virtview, please."

The room darkened instantly and a virtual holographic map of the U.S. appeared at the end of the conference room. Secretary McGuire again led the discussion.

"The red pinpoints on the map," there were maybe ten of them, "represent the areas of greatest concern at the moment. Here in Chicago," and the image jumped to a street level view, "the fighting around the stockyards has been disturbingly intense."

As she spoke, Selling watched U.S. soldiers firing from the protection offered by tanks parked in front of a seemingly endless vista of cattle pens and cows. That they were being fired upon was clear as well because the soldiers kept reacting to rounds ricocheting off the armored vehicles.

"The numbers of persons firing on our forces is quite large here and we are essentially in a siege situation as we attempt to protect the cattle from those who seem intent on releasing them."

The scene shifted back to the large map and McGuire's pointer went to somewhere on Iowa, and the scene jumped again.

"This is, or I should say was, Reynolds Pork and Lard. RPL was the largest supplier of pork products in the world. Last year they grossed over $17 billion. They were a major contributor to this administration's presidential campaign."

Selling saw burnt rubble. A few dead pigs and a few dead humans lay scattered around in the smoking ruins. A number of people were picking their way through the debris and occasionally kneeling down at one of the bodies. A man put a pistol to the head of a pig and fired. Smoke rose from everything and created a hazy and eerie scene.

"We understand that a group of nearly a hundred people dressed in black descended on the facility three nights ago and shot all the workers they could find. Over a two-day period nearly ten thousand pigs were stolen. One of the workers who had been able to hide in a grain bin finally escaped and called the authorities. The bodies and fire are a result of the ensuing clash.

"Jenny," said the president, and the lights in the room came back on and the hologram vanished. "I think you can see, Richard," the president was famous for calling people by their first names and always encouraged others to call him John, "that your, excuse me, Selling's, new animal TE's have caused a real problem. Reports are rolling in from all over about many, though smaller, situations than the two I just showed you. Our people tell us the situation seems to be worsening and that, if we don't do something soon, that things might just spin out of control, and I don't think we want that, no sir, now do we?" The president looked at Selling.

Richard Selling was not used to having others tell him what to think. His willingness to brook the rules of the road had catapulted Selling Inc. into the world's largest mass marketer of consumer electronics and home furnishings in the world. As populations continued to rise, in spite of expert opinions that they were due to level off soon, ever more consumers demanded the newest this and that. Selling Inc. stood out as the company offering the newest and latest of everything.

Two nights earlier, through a blind-brokered deal, Selling had quietly sold every share of every stock in his private portfolio remotely connected to the animal agriculture industry. Selling had sat and experienced all ten animal TEs one after the other. He had variously been a dog, a cat, a cow, a pig on the way to slaughter, a parrot living in a cage, a chimpanzee in a zoo, a city rat – this was an especially interesting experience as the rat was recorded in an underground lair, an elephant in a wildlife park—no really wild areas remained on land any longer, a dolphin in the Pacific, and a chicken.

Following the nearly twenty-hour emersion in the minds of other species, Spelling knew that the world had become a different place, that he had become a different person, that everything was going to be much different in the very near future.

"So, in order to try and reel in the problems you see being associated with the animal TEs you are going to publicly punish me."

"No, no, not you Richard," the president smiled compassionately, "but we have to set an example; we have to let people know that the government is reacting, that we are in control, that everything is OK. More than anything we have to let the food producers see that we will protect their interests and that they don't have to worry about this new fad."

Selling sat quietly for a moment. "Mr. President. John. Have you experienced the animal TEs yourself yet?"

President Adams looked at Selling, cleared his throat, and glanced almost imperceptibly toward the secretary of state.

McGuire answered without pause, "We don't believe that it is in the nation's best interests for the president's health to be placed at risk for the sake of entertainment. It's a sacrifice he's had to make for the people of the United States."

Selling had kept his attention on Adams as McGuire had spoken for him. The politician's smile had not wavered.

"I've had a full report from my advisors, Richard. I know all about these recordings. I can't see what more is to be gained by seeing them myself."

Selling finally looked over at McGuire. Their eyes locked. "What do you mean by *risk*, Ms. McGuire?"

"We are aware of associated mental illness from the use of Selling TEs. Our experts have prepared a report that shows that there is a real and significant risk from exposure to these recordings…"

"All the TEs? Or just the animal TEs?"

McGuire looked toward the attorney general.

Attorney General Wilkins stepped in with careful noncommittal, "Our analysis is incomplete at this time, but we are certain there are risks. We are working to determine the best way to proceed. The public's interest is our paramount concern."

Selling understood now. They wanted to keep the public engaged with the TEs to relieve their mass boredom with life, but wanted at the same time, to stop them from experiencing the world through the mind of an animal. And to do this, they were going to claim that the animal TEs caused mental illness. He wondered how they planned to keep people from experiencing them.

"Have any of you experienced the animal TEs?" Selling asked them.

Wilkins and McGuire looked toward each other, seemingly unsure of who should answer. Finally, the secretary said, "I experienced the cow TE. It was clear to me immediately that it posed a national security risk. I think it unconscionable that such products would be placed on the market. I recommended to the president that immediate steps be taken to stop the production of all the animal TEs and further recommended that you be placed under arrest for attempting to undermine the political stability of the United States. My grandparents were ranchers in Montana, you've made a mockery of everything good about their life."

The room was quiet. The president seemed to have lost some of his smile. Finally, he said, "Yes, well, John. I'm sure you can sense Rebecca's concern and passion for her family and the American way of life. As you can see we are well informed and are trying to do what's best for the country."

Chapter 9

Karen called in sick on Monday. It was the first time she had missed a day at the Enzyme Interaction Institute since getting her dream job. She was sitting on the floor, leaning against the wall in the bedroom of her small apartment. The room was dark. Harlow, a large orange cat, was curled on the pillow that Karen had in her lap. His fur was damp and salty.

Except for trips to the bathroom and filling Harlow's bowls with fresh water and kibble, Karen had been sitting in the same spot for two days. Her TE was lying next to her, the net was on her head. She pressed play, and for the one hundred and fourteenth time since her first experience Saturday evening, Karen became a rat.

She knew the two rats next to her, but the other rat was a stranger and everyone was on edge. He smelled friendly, and his nervousness was obvious. One of the rats with her had a litter of babies hidden away and she was very concerned about the stranger. Whiskers were twitching and everyone was sizing up the situation carefully and keeping all the escape routes in mind. It was pitch dark and Karen couldn't see a thing. The experience was entirely olfactory, tactile, and auditory.

Karen inched carefully toward the stranger until their whiskers were touching. She could smell other strange rats on him but knew that he had not been around them for many days. She sensed that he had been separated from his colony in some way and was seeking the company of other rats now. His squeaks and slow movement told her that he was intending no harm.

The other two rats slowly came forward and began smelling the stranger more carefully. Karen could sense a slight relaxation in the female's wariness. Suddenly the other rat jumped on the stranger and they tussled briefly, but the stranger endured the nips and kicks with little resistance.

They crowed around him and nibbled the fur on his back and licked his anus. He remained still and did not struggle.

They all remained quiet for a time, then went together to look for something to eat.

The first few times Karen had experienced the rat TE, she had been very confused. There was nothing at all to see. As she ran the TE over again, she began to be aware of the meaning of the scents and sounds. She learned that there were things on the TE that were not so apparent the first few times she experienced it.

She could now recognize that the rat she was experiencing knew things about the other rats and his environment that seemed almost subconscious. The rat had a mental map of the tunnels he was in that Karen recognized as a system of drainpipes. He knew which ones led to the streets and where the dumpsters were in relation to the storm drain exits. He knew where there was water and where he had to be especially wary due to other rats' territories. He knew safe places to hide and soft warm places to sleep. He knew where he had hidden little morsels for latter snacking.

Though she never could tell for certain, she didn't think that he had names for the other rats, but it was clear that he knew them and knew things about them. He seemed to trust some and to be nervous about others. He knew that the rat with the litter of babies was his sister.

The most startling thing to Karen had been her eventual recognition of the sympathy and empathy that the rat felt for the stranger. The rat, and the other two rats with him, recognized that the stranger had been alone for a while and that he was lonely and frightened.

None of these things had been apparent to Karen the first time she had experienced the rat TE, and each time she ran it again, she picked up more subtlety and information.

After Karen's third experience a wave of fearful understanding washed over her as she thought of the hundreds of thousands of hamsters and guinea pigs stored in their plastic boxes at the Enzyme Interaction Institute. Their stark plastic cells, their confinement, the many painful procedures they were being subjected to, it all added up to a horror that Karen realized she was contributing to. Her growing self-loathing led her to experience the rat TE again, and then again and again. Her eventual tears had soaked the pillow on her lap as she buried her head and sought to muffle her sobs from the neighbors on the other side of the thin walls of her apartment. Harlow sensed her hurt and had been on her lap for most of the weekend, his back catching many of Karen's salty tears.

Chapter 10

When Harry drove up, the small crowd in front of Vivaldi's Delicatessen was being pushed back by uniformed officers who were stringing a bright yellow ribbon around the area in front of the entrance. Warning! Police Line! Do Not Cross! shouted the bold black block letters over and over again. Harry nodded to one of the officers and stepped over the ribbon and into the store. He quickly surveyed the scene.

The Risks of Empathy

Two women's bodies were sprawled on the floor in pools of blood. A man's body appeared to have crashed backwards through the glass front of a food case. He was dressed in white and had a large dark red hole in his chest. His head was twisted sideways and lying in a large bowl of three-bean salad. A cash register drawer was open behind the counter. An officer was taking notes and talking to a man sitting on the floor against a wall. The man was splattered with blood and had his arm around a young boy who looked to be in shock.

"So what do we know?" Harry asked.

"How the hell are ya Mahoney?" answered the officer who looked up from his inspection of one of the women on the floor.

"Could be better. Was it a robbery?"

"No. At least not a planned robbery, as far as we can tell. The man and his son," nodding toward the man and boy against the wall, "were standing in line behind these two women when another man and a woman came in and immediately started talking loudly about murder and the meat in the window. Apparently, Mr. Vivaldi," nodding toward the man in the case, "came around from behind the counter and started shouting back and tried to push the man out of the store. The witness is a little confused about where the gun came from, but says that the woman with the man screamed something, and Mr. Vivaldi turned toward her and she shot him."

"How did the women get shot?" asked Harry.

"The guy says that the man took the gun from the woman then and said something about cannibals and murder and maybe revenge and shot the two women, one after the other. The witness says he pleaded for his son's life and tried to shield the boy. The next thing he recalled was the police sirens. He said he never noticed the couple leaving because he had his eyes closed."

Harry looked around and noticed the ever-present video camera over the door. "Has anyone pulled the disc yet?"

"Not yet, but I saw the recorder under the counter."

Harry walked around, careful not to step in the blood, ejected the small disc and put it in his pocket. He walked back from around the counter and looked once again around the small store. In the cold case, next to the man with his head in the bean salad, were plates of sausages, long pepperonis, an olive loaf, a couple roasted chickens, a pig's head with an apple in it's mouth, a sliced beef tongue, a pan of ground lamb with a small sign stuck into it proclaiming its great age and high fat content.

Behind the counter a quarter of a beef hung alongside strings of dried sausages. A blackboard announced the prices of everything in yellow chalk. Someone had drawn flowers down one side and colored them with red, blue and green.

Harry noticed that one of the women had a bag under one arm, and a white butcher paper package had fallen out. He imagined the cutlets wrapped inside that she was taking home to prepare for dinner.

The officer said to Harry, "This is the third case like this I had this week. It's odd as hell. I liked the jumpers better; at least I didn't worry about someone going berserk afterwards. Now, I worry about my wife and kids all the time. She's always shopping. What do you think's going on?"

Harry had an idea. "Have you seen the animal TEs?"

The officer seemed confused for a second, seemed to shake it off, and answered, "No, but I really like that football quarterback one, have you done it yet?"

Harry shook his head.

"My brother sent me some with this hot little redhead chick in them...."

Harry shook his head and the officer cut it short, sensing that he had missed the point and maybe offended Harry at the same time.

"Make sure I get your report," was all Harry said.

An ambulance arrived just as Harry was leaving the delicatessen. Since no one had been in need of immediate life-saving care, the medical people had taken their time getting there. Harry nodded to them and heard one comment to the other, "I'm getting sick of all these meat market murders."

Chapter 11

In its heyday HtH Cattle and Timber had been the largest range-fed beef-producing outfit west of the Atlantic Ocean. Its one hundred seventeen thousand acres was massive by any standards even if much of it was arid semi-desert. Its grandiose size gave it its name, Horizon to Horizon, and the original owner liked to falsely boast that the sun never set on HtH.

The property's size made parts of it very remote and generally unknown, even to its neighboring ranchers. There was a small valley near the center of the property that was protected by mountains on three sides. A small spring-fed stream came out of the mountains, ran through the valley, and formed a small lake that marked the valley's edge. The small lake slowly evaporated in the dry air of the desert at just about the same rate that the stream kept it filled. In the valley, between the mountains and the lake, nature had contrived to create a microclimate that pine trees and firs found to their liking. Native grasses clung to life as they competed with the exotic grasses that had taken over the West. All in all, the valley was green, cool in the summer, surprisingly mild in the winter, and home to many animals.

It was in this valley, twenty years ago, that Richard Selling had built his hideaway. He had bought HtH because of the valley. He had mentioned his purchase to very few people, had bought it through a shell company that quietly transferred title to him just before it went out of business, and to the degree he was able to, he had kept the location very private.

The cabin, as Selling referred to it, was simple but sophisticated. The cabin's south façade was mostly glass and overlooked the lake and the desert beyond. It acted as a solar collector and helped warm the building during the cold months of winter. The other rooms had views of mountains and forests reaching up into them; snow clung to the mountaintops throughout much of the summer, offering a cooling vista on hot summer days. The cabin appeared to have grown in place. Its worn silvered wood exterior had been chosen carefully to blend in with the terrain and surrounding forest; the shingles were dark and lined with moss. Two chimneys rose from the roof. They were made of stone that matched the color of the peaks guarding the valley. From the air, it was easy to overlook the cabin due to its easy fit in the valley, just as Selling had wanted it to be.

As gentle and nondescript as the cabin was from the outside, it was state of the art telecommunications and security on the inside. Two of Selling Inc.'s geosynchronous communication satellites relayed continuous data streams to the cabin from news outlets around the world. A third satellite, listed as space junk in all the federal and commercial catalogs, maintained a dedicated comlink with the rest of the planet's communication system via highly encrypted code. As much as Selling enjoyed his semi-reclusive lifestyle, Selling Inc. had become a giant in world commerce specifically because Selling himself kept a watchful eye on the economic and political climate of the market and could respond instantly when need be.

Now, two weeks to the day after he had listened to the White House's excuses for why they were going to put Selling Inc. out of business, Richard Selling sat in his cabin and watched the news from around the world on seven holoscreens; five of them were all saying pretty much the same thing: the United States government had banned the Selling TE, had criminalized sale of Selling TEs, was blocking all Selling TE transmissions, was warning current users against their use due to the discovery that extended exposure to the transmissions would cause irreparable dementia over time, that the Government had set up an exchange program to replace the Selling product with a safe government-tested version, and that there was no cause for alarm unless users had already begun to experience the headaches that were the first sign of the progressive irreparable dementia, and finally, that clinics were being supplied with a vaccine that could reverse the earliest damage, if caught in time. Medics were standing by at all government sanctioned clinics.

The other two holoscreens were featuring the collapse of Selling Inc's stock price.

The old recliner's stuffing had made piece with Rita's curves and bulges many years ago; they fit together as neatly as a body and its skin.

She was walking along the Boulevard de Raspail in Paris, just window shopping and taking in the foreign scents and language. She had gotten over the strangeness of recognizing the meaning of foreign words sometime ago. She drifted into a little coffee shop on a corner, ordered an espresso at the counter and took it outside to a small table and sat watching the foot traffic on the busy street. Students walked by, a woman selling flowers, shoppers with bags filled with packages, fresh produce peeking out. Music was wafting through the warm light breeze. She picked up the small demitasse and inhaled the rich aroma and ... suddenly, she was no longer in Paris, but was instead standing in a featureless room with a fairly attractive middle aged man in a gray suit standing in from of her.

"Don't be alarmed," he said. "We apologize for the sudden intrusion. My name is Dr. Frank Jones, I represent the U.S. Virtual Broadcasting Network.

"The Surgeon General has determined that the Selling Total Experience transmissions may be hazardous to your health. In the interest of public safety, the government will replace all Selling TEs with government tested and approved virtual experiences. This new service will be provided by the U.S. Virtual Broadcasting Network. It is our sincere desire to provide you with the best in safe virtual experience.

"Your Selling TE receiver may be exchanged, free of charge, for a new VBN receiver at any government broadcasting office.

"All Selling TE receivers and any broadcast recordings must be replaced within seventy-two hours. If you are unable to visit a U.S. Virtual Broadcasting Network office in person, your Selling TE receiver may be deposited in any U.S. Postal mail deposit box along with a postcard with the receiver's serial number and your signature.

"As of January 1, 2160, personal possession or viewing of the Selling TE will be deemed a Class A Felony. Conviction of this offense may result in a $5,000 fine, imprisonment of up to fives years in a federal penitentiary, or both. Sale or other distribution of a Selling TE receiver or a recording of a Selling TE may be punishable by a $10,000 fine or imprisonment of up to ten years in a federal penitentiary, or both.

"I apologize again, for the intrusion. All Selling TE transmissions are hereby cancelled by order of the Surgeon General.

"The U.S. Virtual Broadcasting Network looks forward to serving you and providing you with entertaining and safe virtual experiences in the future. Thank you."

There was a slight flicker and he began again, "Don't be alarmed. We apologize for the sudden intrusion. My name is Dr. Frank Jones, I represent the Surgeon General of the United States of America..."

Rita reached down to the receiver in her lap and changed the channel, "Don't be alarmed. We apologize for the sudden intrusion ...".

he worked her way through the channels and found the same dull gray room and the same dull monologue on every one. Rita leaned the recliner forward and sat for awhile wondering about the message. She glanced over at the old clock hanging on the wall and decided she might as well walk down to Jim's Lounge.

Chapter 12

The backlash began almost immediately. An underground network dealing in copies of Selling TEs and Selling TE receiver clones popped into existence almost before the government got their replacement broadcasts on the air. Just like the old days when alcohol and narcotics were illegal, prohibition brought with it a black-market bonanza. Prior to the ban, black-marketers were dealing only in the seediest recordings: murders, rapes, torture; and the market was limited to the same sliver of humanity that has always found such immorality scintillating.

And, as with all the other failed attempts at prohibition, its result was the exposure of good people to the dark undercurrents of human behavior, crime, and depravity.

And people were recognizing that the truth behind the Selling ban had nothing to do with any medical risk; the ban was aimed entirely at limiting access to the Selling animal TEs.

And more people were pointing this out.

And more people were asking questions.

And the government's credibility was further undermined.

And the violence spread....

The open stock truck turned off the shimmering asphalt highway onto a gravel road and stopped. The road showed the effects of much recent travel. A washboard of gravel and dust stretched into the distance ahead and pointed toward a range of mountains with their peaks still brushed with snow.

Two camouflage fatigue-dressed people with mean-looking assault weapons in their hands appeared and approached the truck, one on the driver's side and one on the passenger side. Their faces were hidden by the netting that hung down from their helmets.

The window on the driver's side lowered and a woman leaned out. "Hey, how y'all doin'? These guys must be mighty thirsty by now. I need to get 'em some water pretty soon."

In the back of the truck fifty or so obviously nervous ostriches were crammed together. Their eyes were wide and they were all panting.

"Sarah," said the guard on her side, "I can't believe you make these runs alone. You're just asking for trouble." The guard pulled the netting up over his helmet and gave her a big grin. " Get these guys out of here."

And with that, the ostriches began the last bumpy leg of their journey to refuge within the reaches of the HtH Timber and Cattle Company.

Chapter 13

Karen placed her hand on the palm reader and heard the door's automatic lock slide open. She held the door as the five darkly clad figures slipped inside. She knew, and had told them earlier, that there was nothing she could do about the video surveillance in the halls.

She led them quietly and surely to the security center where one of them placed a small plastic explosive on the door, even as the guard inside was calling for help on the intercom. The door blew open, two people rushed inside and Karen heard a muffled pop. She never heard a word from the guard.

The Risks of Empathy

Karen left them and ran through the hall to the employee locker room to grab her few belongings. As she was passing Yu's office, the door opened and the scientist looked out to see what was causing the commotion. Without thought and not knowing why she was doing it, she put her hand on Yu's chest and pushed him back into the office and closed the door behind her.

"You better stay in here Dr. Yu. There are terrorists in the building, and I think someone's already been hurt."

Yu looked at Karen with some confusion, then he seemed to understand what she said.

"Yes. I will stay here. Security must be called."

"They've been called already, Dr. Yu."

Karen and Yu heard shouts and what sounded like a gun. "I don't know what these people are thinking," said Yu. "This is a scientific laboratory. We are scientists!"

"We'd better hide! Let's get under your desk," said Karen as she pulled out the chair.

Yu and Karen got down on their hands and knees and crawled into the space under Yu's large desk. They were both fairly small, and once under the desk, they had room to sit across from each other. It was close and intimate, but they weren't crushed together. They heard more shouts and more gunshots. Karen noticed that Yu was sweating and that his normally immaculate combed-back black hair had become a bit disheveled. Yu seemed to be aware of this and kept trying to smooth his hair down by using his fingers as a comb. His hand was getting oilier with every pass through this hair.

"If we just stay here I am sure we will be safe," said Yu, but his jerky response to the noises that seemed now to be coming from the hall outside and the floor above belied his spoken assurance.

"What do they want, Dr. Yu? Why are they here?" asked Karen, wondering what was going through Yu's mind.

"They are the animal people," said Yu, as if this answered everything.

"But what do they want, doctor?"

"The animals. They think the animals are people. They are crazy. It is those animal TEs."

"What are you talking about?"

"Haven't you seen them? Karen? Your name is Karen?" Yu seemed finally to realize who she was.

"Yes Dr. Yu. I'm your lab assistant, Karen Brown. I've been your assistant for the past four months."

"Of course, " said Yu. "Sometimes I have a hard time remembering names. You are the one who asked me about liver transplants."

"That's right, but no, I haven't seen the animal TEs," Karen lied. "Have you? What are they like?"

Yu looked at his knees folded and just touching Karen's. "They are... interesting, but little more. I watched one about a rat. The rat was in the dark, it was a dull creature, there was a fight with another rat. It meant nothing."

"I heard there were many of them," she coaxed.

"Yes. There were nine made. Dog, cat, cow, pig, chimpanzee, rat, elephant, dolphin, and chicken. I watched them all."

"So they were nothing?" asked Karen.

Yu kept his attention on their knees. He continued to readjust his coiffure. He appeared to be in meditation.

"Dr. Yu?"

Yu started and seemed to refocus on Karen's question. "The chimpanzee was a little surprising. She was alone and seemed almost unaware of all the people who walked by her cage. She thought of the forest and seemed to remember other chimpanzees that might have once been her family. She didn't seem to realize that she chewed on her arm all of the time."

Yu cleared his voice and bumped his head on the bottom of the desk when a small explosion shook the building gently.

"One thing that surprised me was that she seemed to be able to read a little..."

"What do you mean?"

"Well, this is odd, but she knew that the popcorn boxes said popcorn on them. It wasn't that she knew there was popcorn in the boxes, which she did, but that she actually read the word. She heard 'popcorn' in her mind when she took the time to notice the people starring at her and what was in their hands. It was very human-like."

Karen didn't know what to say, and didn't know why she was under the desk with Yu. "Aren't there monkeys here at the Institute?"

Yu snapped to. "Yes. Of course there are. We are using them in the transplantation experiments. You know that."

"Well, after what you have told me about the chimpanzee..." her voice quavered slightly, "don't you think that, maybe, we shouldn't be using them in the experiments?"

Yu looked Karen in the eyes, "We are scientists. Even if these animals are like us, what does that matter? We must learn. We must progress. We are human they are animal!"

Yu's eyes seemed to be bugging out, he had given up on his hair; a small bit of spittle was foaming in the corner of his mouth. Karen thought he was about to explode when the door burst open and a guard was shouting into the room, "Dr Yu! Dr. Yu! Are you in here?"

Yu yelled back, "Yes we are here!"

Yu crawled out first and Karen heard the guard say, "It was one of the junior scientists who let them in, most of the animals are gone."

Karen crawled out behind Yu, and bolted through the door as the guard yelled after her, "Hey! That's her! Stop her!"

But she was gone and down the hall and out the door before anyone could. A dark car drove up and she jumped through the open door into the back seat. The door slammed shut and the car drove away at an unconcerned and unremarkable pace. Harlow crawled into her lap and began to purr; a voice from the front said, "Good job. We wondered why you took so long though. Try to get some rest now. We won't get to the ranch until morning."

Chapter 14

Richard Selling had recognized the risk to Stan and Earnie as soon as he understood the government's intention toward the animal TEs. Selling had the inventors moved quietly into a new, well-hidden laboratory. When federal agents swooped in to take the scientists into custody, all they found was an empty building and a single TE recording disc.

Karen awoke when the sedan hit the rough road. The slight odor coming from the litter box down on the floorboard made her think of Harlow, and she started as she realized he wasn't lying on or next to her. Her slight worry disappeared as she sat up and saw the big orange cat curled up between the two people in the front seat. Out her window she saw sagebrush reaching to the horizon, while the other window and the front windshield framed forested mountains.

Karen turned and looked out the rear window and saw that they were being followed by large truck.

"How much longer?" Karen asked.

"Well, good morning," said the passenger who turned and put out her hand to Karen. "It'll be a couple more hours before we reach the camp, but we'll stop at one of the rodent barns first. My name's Sarah."

Karen shook her hand and caught the driver's eye in the rearview mirror. The man nodded to her and said, "I'm Harry. Harry Mahoney," but kept his eyes on the ruts and stones in the road.

Sarah leaned over and hit Harry in the shoulder. "Harry's an ex-cop. All business. You'll get used to him."

Karen looked out the window again saw half a dozen silhouettes on a low hill. "I think I just saw some ostriches!"

"It could have been the emus," said Sarah, "but they probably were ostriches. There are almost two hundred here now. They've been pretty easy to rescue. Most of the big ranches don't have guards and the birds are really docile at night and are easily herded into a truck. They seem to like it here, but I don't think anyone has listened in to one of them yet. Have they Harry?"

"I don't know," answered Harry.

They drove around another low hill and then stopped. Karen noticed that the road had stopped abruptly and she wondered what was going on. "I though we were stopping at a barn."

"This is it," said Sarah and as she was explaining that the hill in front of them was actually the top of a dome sunken into the earth, a large door opened and they drove into an expansive room that appeared to be a warehouse. The truck pulled in behind them and the door slid shut.

"You worked with rodents in that lab, didn't you Karen?" asked Sarah. "Come on, I'll show you around. You're going to love this."

"But what about Harlow?"

"He seems to like me OK," answered Harry. "He can hang out here with me until you get back."

As they walked along people said hello to Sarah and she introduced Karen to many of them. Karen saw carts loaded with plastic boxes with pale blue lids. The boxes held guinea pigs and hamsters and were being pushed along and toward a set of double doors. "Those are some of the animals you helped rescue, Karen," said Sarah. "These guys were on a truck ahead of us. They'll be quarantined and spayed before they are released into population. Come on."

They stepped into a small room and the door closed behind them. A lock clicked, and a door on the other side of the room opened. "We have a double door system to keep them from getting out, but some of the little buggers manage to escape every now and then no matter what we do," laughed Sarah. "Watch where you step."

The Risks of Empathy

A dirt path greeted them as the entered, and almost immediately a small brown body scurried across and along a much narrower path that disappeared into the grass. "Let's sit over here," said Sarah and led them to a wooden bench. As soon as they sat down two squirrels appeared and one of them jumped up on the bench. "There's a rule about not hand-feeding them, but it's pretty clear that not everyone follows it."

The squirrel sat for a while, seemed to give up and jumped down and vanished into the grass with the other squirrel close behind.

Karen was surprised by the sheer size of the park. Park seemed to describe it best. There were bushes, small trees, paths and well-mown grass. She noticed holes and little mounds of earth here and there. "Are those burrows?" she asked.

"Yes. The gerbils, hamsters, ground squirrels, and rabbits all burrow. The rats prefer to nest in the buildings, and the guinea pigs have nest boxes."

"What buildings?"

"Come on. Remember to watch your step."

As the women walked along the path, Sarah explained that the grass, which really wasn't mowed after all, and small plants, served to feed most of the dome's residents, but that grains and fruits were provided daily. Water flowed through a small shallow artificial stream, but sprinklers provided "rain" two days a week and kept the plants lush. The light was artificial. A population of flies, ants and other insects had established themselves and were eaten by some of the rodents.

"How many animals are in here?" asked Karen as two more squirrels stopped in the path and seemed to check out the possibility that the women had treats.

"About a hundred thousand in this barn. There is another barn about the same size nearby, but the big barn holds almost a million."

"Oh my God. I never imagined..."

"We don't have room for them all. Mr. Selling is trying to establish other sanctuaries around the world, but the number of refugees surpasses anything we might be able to provide. It's a real mess, and the fucking labs, the ones that haven't been burnt down yet, keep breeding more. No one knows what we are going to do."

A small flock of birds zipped by Karen's head. "What in the world?"

"They're larks. Some asshole was experimenting on their brains trying to discover how they learn their songs. He raised some in complete isolation and discovered that if they don't learn their songs early in life that they can't learn them later on. Big deal. Just what we need to know. There're about thirty of them in here. We didn't know what else to do with them. They don't know how to live in the wild anymore, but they seem to relish flying. Here're the rat buildings."

Buildings seemed like a funny word for the things Karen was looking at, but she could not think of a better one. The rat buildings were about six feet high and seemed to have nine or ten stories or levels. They were made of wood and no two looked alike. A new one was under construction. Karen saw balconies and holes in the walls leading to inner compartments. Some were blind alleys and some were interconnected. It was a village, or town with about a hundred or so of the buildings arranged rather randomly. Arial walkways connected some of them. The odor was exquisite.

"They are constantly gnawing and remodeling. We give them a new one every so often. Look over here." Sarah walked through the town and stopped at one of the, apparently, older buildings.   "I know the rat who lives here, unless he's moved." She looked down at her watch, "It's still a little early-you won't believe how busy it gets in here at night; except for some of the squirrels, almost everyone is nocturnal, but Ratty might be willing to get up if he recognizes my voice."

Sarah knocked on one of the walls. She looked into a dark hole and called gently, "Ratty. Are you in there? Come see me."

A moment later a black nose appeared and twitched this way and that. A large black rat stepped out on the balcony, stretched, yawned widely displaying his long yellow teeth, and walked over to Sarah and sniffed her nose. "There you are!" said Sarah as she stroked his body. She put out her hand, and with no hesitation the rat crawled into her hand, up her arm and onto her shoulder. She took him in both hands and kissed him on top of the head. "Want to hold him?" she said to Karen and offered the rat to her.

Karen had understood, both intellectually and emotionally, the implications of the rat TE she had experienced over and over again in her apartment. Her understanding had led to her willingness to help these people break into Yu's facility and rescue as many of the animals as they could. But she had never handled a rat or even a hamster or a guinea pig for any reason other than picking one up to break its neck. This big black rat that seemed anxious to get to her, frightened her. "I don't know if..." she began, but it was too late. Sarah pushed the rat to her, and without effort the rat crawled up her chest and on to her shoulder and began rooting around in her hair and sniffing her ear. Karen was frozen.

Sarah watched for a few moments, seemed to understand Karen's reaction, and took the rat back. "He's great isn't he?" She set him on the balcony in front of his hole. He yawned again. "Come scratch his side. He loves it."

Sarah showed Karen where he liked to be ticked and Karen summoned up the courage to scratch the big rat. As she scratched around his ears and on top of his head, he closed his eyes and seemed to drift off. She thought back to her days in the lab, looked around rat town and around the park and then to the small animal who was trusting her to scratch his neck. Her life had taken a large u-turn.

"We better go," said Sarah, "you'll need to get your stuff and grab Harlow before we find you a place to bed down." The she reached into her pocket and pulled out a peanut still in the shell.

"Here, give him this, but don't tell anyone," she grinned. "By the way, if you come back here on your own later on, be very careful around the rats. Most of them will bite you as soon as look at you. Rat bites hurt like hell." She kissed Ratty on top of the head, said goodbye, and led Karen back along the path.

Chapter 15

Ted had learned to be unconcerned with the various things that Stan put on his head. Stan had never hurt him and he liked the attention. Earnie manipulated dials and Stan tried to relax and think happy thoughts. Ted seemed oblivious.

"I wonder how we would even be sure that he was getting something?" mused Stan. "I mean, unless there's food or a walk involved, Ted's pretty laid back."

The big dog sat up and looked at Stan. He cocked his head to one side and panted twice. Earnie broke the connection.

"I think he got something!"

Earnie scratched his head, "I don't know. Ted! Ted!" and Ted looked over at Earnie, cocked his head and let his tongue loll out.

"See. I mean, how can we tell?"

"Hook him up! Jeez, we're idiots." And in just a few moments Ted was fitted with a recording net on his head, over the receiving headband. As Ted was supposed to be receiving Stan's thoughts, Earnie would be hooked into Ted's as he received Stan's.

"Do it again."

Stan and Earnie had worried about the effect on Ted if he got swallowed into a human's mental experience with no forewarning, so they had agreed that Stan should try to relax and think simple comfortable thoughts.

Earnie was Ted. And he was Ted just realizing that he was Stan. Stan ran his fingers through his hair and Earnie/Ted remembered running down a hill laughing as Stan remembered a childhood episode.

Memories are always recorded dreamily and gauze-like.

Harry Mahoney was sitting under a pine tree on a bench. A large pig was stretched out in the sun near his feet. Harry watched an odd herd of horses, donkeys, goats, and ostriches grazing peacefully on the top of a nearby hill. He thought back to the butcher shop and the decision he had made.

Harry wasn't an animal lover, and he had viewed the first animal TE out of curiosity. But Harry was kind and ethical. Harry was moral.

He had stopped at the first trash auto-incinerator he had come upon. He noticed the ubiquitous trash scattered up and down the street and mused to himself that the incinerators were not getting used enough. He pulled the door open and tossed in the surveillance tape he had taken from the crime scene at the delicatessen. He knew that he was incinerating his career even as the videodisc was turning to ash. Harry couldn't understand why anyone would or could hurt an animal after living a bit of their life. Harry couldn't understand the fact that the government was allowing it all to continue. When he heard the news about banning the Selling TEs, he had realized the position that the government was going to take, and he also knew that he would never be able do anything but support any effort to stop the carnage. It had been just a matter of time before he was forced to make an ethical choice that was contrary to the interests of the state.

Harry remembered the slight scent of vaporized plastic videodisc. He remembered taking out his wallet and pulling out his police identification card. He had looked at it, put it to his nose and breathed in its own distinct plastic aroma. He had put it back in his wallet realizing that it might come in handy sometime.

Harry startled back to his bench when the pig let out a grunt. It looked to Harry like the pig was dreaming.

President John Adams was sitting on a small comfortable couch in his bedroom. He had a terrycloth robe on over his pajamas. His wife Betty was next to him in her own soft flannel robe. The president was leaning

145

against her lightly, enjoying her familiar warmth and scent. They both had their feet up on the Louis XIV coffee table. Betty had a glass of white wine and President Adams was nursing a beer.

"You're going to have to see for yourself, John," said Betty.

"I've already been told about them, Bet. The experts told me tha..."

"Experts my ass! There are no experts in this. This is new territory John. You have to experience this for yourself."

"They say there're risks, Bet. I don't think you should use them either."

Betty shrugged her shoulder pushing her husband away. She put her feet down squarely on the floor and wheeled on him and looked him squarely in the eye. "You listen to me. Your experts can all go to hell. I'm telling you. I'm not asking. Look at the damn things."

The First Lady rarely ordered her husband to do anything, but John Adams had learned and accepted long ago that his wife had him easily beaten in the smarts department, and when she was sure about something, she was usually right.

Chapter 16

Since Karen's arrival at the ranch, she had been working in the rodent houses. She had continued her relationship with Ratty, the large black rat Sarah had introduced her to on that first day so many weeks ago.

Karen was lying on the grass among the rat buildings; the large rat was nuzzling through her hair and sticking his nose in her ear.

Karen laughed and tickled the rat on his side. She figured he was laughing in the high pitch that humans could not hear. She sat up and the rat crawled into her lap and up the sleeve of her shirt. With her attention on Ratty, she did not notice the young-looking man who walked up and sat down on the grass next to her without an invitation.

"Aren't you the woman from the lab?" he asked.

"That's right. Who are you?"

"I'm Earnie."

At the ranch, Stan and Earnie had become legends. Everyone knew that it was they who had invented TEs and who had first thought to find out what animals were thinking with the experience recordings.

"Stan and Earnie?"

"Yep. One of the famous guys," he answered. "Who's your friend?"

Ratty was sticking his head out of Karen's sleeve wiggling his nose and feelers trying to get a fix on the new voice. "This is my friend Ratty. Ratty, say hello to Earnie," and she held her arm over Earnie's lap.

Ratty turned around in Karen's sleeve, but finally stepped down and began sniffing out this new human.

"So, do you still like science?" asked Earnie as he gently stroked Ratty's paper-thin ears.

"You mean, do I hate science now after realizing the torture I was helping commit in the name of science?"

"Yeah, I guess that's what I mean."

"I love science. I just hate cruelty. Why?"

"Well, we could use some help in our lab, and I wanted to know whether you'd like to help us. We are working on something new."

"What is it?"

Earnie laughed, "It's hard to say exactly, but you won't be bored. You'll have to see for yourself. Listen I gotta go, if you want the job I'll tell Mr. Selling and he'll let security know. Come by the main house in the morning around nine. OK?"

Karen thought for a millisecond and said, "OK."

"Here's your friend back, and he set Ratty back into Karen's lap. As he walked away, he thought that she might be the prettiest girl he had ever seen.

Chapter 17

The tobacco and marijuana smoke was thick in Jim's Lounge. Business had picked up again after the ban on the Selling TEs took hold. The government versions seemed less real somehow, and no one liked the damned commercials that they had started inserting into them. Who wanted to hear about a sale on furniture when you were surfing Pipeline in Hawaii?

Rita sat in a booth with three other regulars. The conversation topics had been the same now for some time: revolution and animals.

"I heard that people are takin' animals out of labs. I heard that people are goin' right in to restaurants and delicatessens and shooting the people selling meat."

Heads shook in agreement. "I wish I had the guts to do that."

"Well, I heard that there're places out west where animals and people are livin' together and startin' their own countries."

"I don't know about that," said Rita. "It seems to me that the government would step right in if people was claiming they was starting a whole new country."

"Look, they ain't sayin' it, but they're sure as hell doin' it."

They all sat quietly for a moment letting the idea sink in.

"What I don't get is why there's no news about this." They all looked over at the vert-view mounted above the bar. A football game was on, but there had been no news about the animals or the underground revolution that everyone everywhere was talking about.

Karen had never been in the main house. Everyone knew that Richard Selling came and went, but he was rarely seen. She walked up the stone steps to the large front porch and started to knock, but the door opened and a man she recognized instantly said, "Hi, you must be Karen. I'm Richard Selling."

Karen was only a little nonplussed by being greeted by Selling; her time at the Enzyme Institute had at least offered her enough experience with meeting famous people that she could now do so without appearing completely befuddled.

"Mr. Selling, I'm so honored to meet you. Nothing I can say can express the admiration I feel for all you have done."

Selling actually blushed and guffawed, "Why anyone in my shoes would have done the same. Now hush, or my head will simply swell too big for this door. Come on in. I'll take you down to the lab."

Selling led Karen through the house to a door that opened to reveal a second steel door behind it. Selling pushed a button next to the door and it slid open revealing the inside of an elevator.

"After you, Karen," he said, and stepped into the elevator with her. He pressed one of only four unlabeled buttons and the floor seemed to drop away. Karen realized that they were going deep underground.

Selling's basic survivalist notions had motivated him to equip the cabin with a keep buried deep within the rock. He had intended it as his retreat of last resort should the world take a particularly lunatic or anarchic turn. During the excavation they had broken through the ceiling of an immense underground cavern that he was still exploring. It had been the obvious place to set up Stan and Earnie's lab once they and their paradigm-shaking research became machina non grata.

The elevator slowed and the doors slid open silently. Karen was unprepared for the magnitude of the expanse that opened before her and she let out a small gasp.

"It catches most visitors off guard," said Selling. "We were really lucky to have found this place. We still don't know how far it extends back into the mountains, but the engineers tell me that we could probably survive even a direct hit from a medium sized nuclear missile. The way things are going, we might have to put it to the test."

Karen took her eyes off the lit cavern and the dark shadows that suggested hidden rooms and corridors to look over at Selling to see whether he was speaking figuratively. The seriousness of his face suggested that he wasn't.

Metal walkways led off in a variety of directions from the elevator and along one of these came two decidedly disheveled men being followed by a large dog.

Karen recognized Earnie who walked up and said, "Hi Richard." He beamed, "Hello Karen, I'm so glad you came! These are my friends Ted and Stan."

Karen reached out and shook hands with Stan and told him what an honor it was to actually be meeting him. She look down at the dog and said, "Hello, Ted."

Ted cocked his head a little and looked over at Stan.

Stan said, "She's OK."

Ted walked up to Karen and sniffed her crotch. He sniffed her legs and let her scratch his neck. He wagged his tail. Earnie said, "Ted thinks you're OK too. Come see the lab. I'll show you what we are trying to do. Richard, are you coming?"

"No," said Selling. "I have some other things I have to take care of right now. I'm sure I'll be seeing you around Karen. Enjoy yourself. Take good care of her you guys, don't scramble her brain." He winked at Karen. "I'll see you later." And he walked off along one of the other metal walkways.

Stan and Ted led the way. Earnie walked with Karen and talked with her about their new project.

"We've been working for a couple of months trying to modify the transduction cells to synchronize with random and unspecified neural frequencies and unpredictable fluctuations of feedback."

"I have no idea what you just said," admitted Karen.

"I'm sorry. I talk to Stan too much. We've been trying to work out a device that will allow us to send and receive thoughts at the same time. Sort of a mental telephone. The problem has been an odd sort of feedback. If you and I were hooked up, I would be getting your thoughts while you were getting mine, but they would be the thought that you are getting my thoughts, so we end up in a sort of endless loop. See?"

"Hum, not really."

"Here we are," announced Stan. They stepped through a door and into a lab that seemed more like a TV repair shop than the modern labs that Karen had worked in at Enzyme. Pieces of electronic equipment, much of which Karen did not recognize, lay ill arranged on work benches and spread around the room. Ted walked over to a large over-upholstered chair in the corner covered in dog hair. It was obviously his standard post.

"The problem is hard to put into words, but the feedback problem is real. When Earnie and I hooked ourselves up we got stuck for about eight hours. If Ted hadn't gotten bored and started licking my face, I have no idea how long we would have been stuck. Want to try it?"

"Well..." began Karen with obviously hesitancy, but Earnie interrupted her.

"There won't be a problem. With Stan here to break the connection, we won't stay hung up. This is why we need another person. We were working with Ted, but it's hard to know whether the problems were with the theory and electronics or because he's a dog." Ted looked up at the mention of his name. "We know that he can experience human experiences, we've seen that, but this feedback problem is really sticky. We need another human. I promise you won't get hurt."

Karen wondered about the effects on Ted of experiencing a human's experience, but he seemed none the worse for it. She wondered about the effects of being 'hung up' with another mind, but Stan and Earnie seemed OK, or at least not too nuts. She let out a little laugh and said, "OK, I'm in. Hook me up."

Chapter 18

President Adams sat in a small sitting room in the White House. A light tap at the door signaled that his guest had arrived. A Marine dressed in a crisply starched uniform let Secretary of State Rebecca McGuire into the room. He closed the door quietly behind her.

"Rebecca. Good evening. Thanks for coming. I hope I haven't caused you too much inconvenience at this late hour of the night."

"You said it was urgent, Mr. President. I came right away. Is there a problem?"

President John Adams was wearing a maroon terrycloth robe and light blue flannel pajamas. His slippers were broken down in the back and had obviously been a part of his nightly wardrobe for a number of years. He had a cup of tea next to him. His ready-for-bed rumpled appearance confused McGuire. She had expected to be escorted to the White House situation room in the basement.

"Sit down Rebecca," said the president motioning to the only other chair in the room and positioned intimately next to his own. "Would you like something to drink? Black oolong isn't it?"

"That would be nice Mr. President. Thanks for remembering." She had the correct impression that whatever Adams intended to discuss he was going to take his time with it. She wondered whether he was considering a shake up of the cabinet; there had been rumors.

Adams picked up the phone next to him and mentioned something about the tea. Almost immediately, a soft knock preceded the door opening. A woman dressed neatly in a dark blue dress came in carrying a small teapot and a cup and saucer on a silver tray. The tea was already steeping and the aroma wafted in behind her on the air current. She sat the tray on the small table between them. She left without saying a word.

"Rebecca," Adams began even as she was pouring the tea from the Wedgwood teapot into the matching small pink cup, "I asked you here because you said during our meeting with Richard Selling, that you had tried out the cow TE and thought that the animal TEs were a threat to national security. Do you remember saying that?"

"Of course Mr. President. That's one of the reasons we banned them."

"Yes, well, just between us. What did you really think of it?"

Patricia McGuire had her sights set on the presidency itself. Her longing for power was the motivation behind everything she did. She rarely said anything without subjecting it to a calculus intended to measure the costs and benefits, the advantages and the risks associated with it. Her statements were closely measured reactions that she felt were the most politic. But sitting with Adams, him in his robe and pajamas, the tea and simple intimacy of the moment, McGuire was uncommonly frank and authentic.

"I don't know what the big deal was. I mean, of course a cow is thinking about something sometime. Why did that surprise anyone? I just don't see what it matters."

"Were you surprised by the similarity between the cow's concern for her calf and a mother's concern for her child?"

"Well, I've never had children, as you know, but my sister, Pam, has two daughters. I'm not that close to them, but I think she loves them a lot. At

151

least she says she does. But, I wasn't that surprised, no. I mean, when you think about it, doesn't it just make sense that a mother is a mother and that she will be concerned for her offspring? So you used the cow TE? I thought we had decided that it was too much of a risk?"

"Betty just made me," chuckled Adams. "Didn't hurt me a bit. And yes, it did surprise me. What did you see as the risk?"

"Actually, sir, Wilkins and I were worried about the effect the animal TEs might have on you. We were worried that you would make a big deal over them and that, if you did, that the economy would be threatened by the major upheaval that would necessarily result if you overreacted. The effect on the world's economy could be disastrous."

"I see."

"Don't take it the wrong way Mr. President. Some people, like yourself, are just very softhearted."

President John Adams sat quietly. McGuire wondered whether he had fallen asleep. She began questioning her rare candor. She checked the teapot and drained it into her cup making a few more clinks of spoon against china than were necessary.

"I'm just thinking Rebecca. I don't see how we can't do something."

Secretary of State, Rebecca McGuire said guardedly, "You're probably right Mr. President," and began plotting her own quick ascendancy to the presidency.

Chapter 19

It was almost as much fun as the real Selling TEs, and it was definitely more exciting. Rita crouched behind the dumpster in dark damp alley. She had a large purse with her that had a distinct petroleum aroma. One of her friends from the bar was crouched next to her. He reached into his back pocket and pulled out a small brown flask. "Here."

Rita took the flask and indulged in a small sip. She usually tried to stay sober and sharp before a raid, but she didn't want to seem rude. "Let's go," she said.

Rita led the way up to the rear of the building and peeped in through the grime-clouded window. Her partner crowded next to her and together they took in the scene. Three people were hard at work cutting up chicken carcasses. Two barrels of plucked chickens stood in the center of the room and a pile of cut and wrapped pieces was growing on a cart nearby.

As a chicken was cut up, wrapped in white paper, and tossed onto the cart, the worker grabbed another from the barrel and began dismembering it.

Rita whispered to her partner, "They keep moving these places, and we keep finding them.." Rita reached into her bag and took out a wine bottle fitted with a cloth stopper.

"Take the hammer. When I say go, smash the window and then run like hell. I'll meet you back at the bar in about an hour. Don't lose the hammer." Rita reached into her pocket, pulled out her cigarette lighter, and lit the Molotov cocktail. "Go!"

...being Earnie being Karen being Earnie being Karen ....

"Karen." Someone was shaking her shoulder and talking to her. She recognized Stan and was wholly back.

"Wow. That was weird as shit. How long were we connected?"

"About three hours. I thought it best to let you see just how impossible it is to break the loop."

When the connection had been established Karen's first fleeting impression had been of being Earnie followed almost immediately with the experience of him realizing he was her realizing she was him. It was like being in a hall of mirrors and seeing one's reflection disappear into infinity. There was nothing to get hold of, no thought had an end because it reverberated back and forth, no new thought could begin because none could finish. Subjectively, there had been no passage of time, just endless re-realizations that she was him realizing that he was realizing her realizing that she was him.

"It's a really hard problem," said Earnie. "It's much harder than anything we've yet had to deal with. If the potential wasn't so high we might just can the whole damn thing."

"Have you tried it with more than just two people?" asked Karen.

"Like a ménage à trois," grinned Earnie. "No, but I don't see how it could hurt. What do you think Stan?"

The entire ranch was aware that things had taken a decidedly difficult turn. The declared martial law was clear on a number of points. First, and foremost, anyone caught with a Selling TE was to be held and tried as a spy and terrorist. The government had fabricated some nonsense about the TEs being used by terrorist cells to communicate with each other. Second, Richard Selling had been named as the likely head of the revolutionary forces and had been moved to the top of the CIA's and the FBI's Most Wanted Lists. Third, anyone caught interfering with any animal based concern—including ranching, fur farming, biomedical research, rodeos, pet stores, restaurants serving meat, stores selling meat, trucks hauling animals to slaughter, packing houses, zoos, aquariums, and any other animal enterprise not specifically named—were to be held as a spy and tried as a terrorist.

Stan and Earnie were as unsettled as the rest of the ranch and told Karen to take a day or two off. Everyone seemed to want to get their hands dirty with the care of the animals. Somehow, taking care of their basic needs seemed to help settle people's anxiety. They all felt there was a storm just over the horizon and coming their way.

Chapter 20

Harry was on his knees with the side of his head down flat on the floor; he was looking under a pallet stacked with bags of cracked corn. He was talking to a small brown mouse. "Come on now. Get out of there. I need to move this corn into the barn."

He looked up and over his shoulder at Karen and said, "Hand me that rake behind the forklift seat."

She did, but said, "Be careful Harry."

Harry used the handle to reach under the pallet and gently nudge the mouse. It ran out and under the next pallet. Harry smiled and got up. "That's about the tenth time I've flushed him. I think he is learning not to be too worried about me."

Karen sat down on one of the forklift's two work-polished tines and breathed a deep sigh.

"What was that for?" asked Harry. "You didn't think I was going to hurt the little guy did you?"

"No, it's just that I've been thinking more about this whole situation. Mr. Selling says we might actually have to fight a real war. I just don't get it. What's wrong with people Harry? Why can't they see the truth? Why don't they care?"

Harry walked around and sat down on the other silver tine. He looked at Karen, seemed to think for a moment, and answered her sigh with one of his own. "Well. Do you want to hear my opinion on the subject?"

"Yes, of course."

"I think that there are four kinds of people in the world. There're those who see immediately that animals are people; I don't mean they're human of course, but some people seem to notice immediately that there's someone looking back at them when they look into a dog's or a cow's eyes. But people like that, people who are sensitive or open enough to see this on their own, well, they're rare. I doubt that many of the people around here are like that. Most of the people around here are in the second group.

"The second kind of person is someone who is shocked that they have been missing something that seems obvious once it's pointed out to them. Or, in this case, it's the kind of person who really is kind and has always been kind and at least a little charitable. These are people like you and me. Once we watched the TEs we realized that we'd just been wrong or had missed the fact that a dog really is a sort of a person. I think these are the kind of a people around here mostly. I think that most people are like this. We are shocked at first because we didn't really imagine that an animal was something very different from anything else we owned or ate like a shoe or a carrot.

"The third kind of person is someone who watches a TE and gets a little shock but is either too stupid or selfish or too something to care. I guess that these are the kind of people who never did really care too much about other people either. So when they learned that a horse was another person, they just said 'so what?'

"That's what I think."

"But you said you think that there are four kinds of people," said Karen.

"Yeah, I guess I did. The fourth group scares me so much that I don't like to think about them. Those are the people who didn't learn anything they didn't already know when they watched an animal TE."

"Like the first group?"

"Sort of," answered Harry. "But these people have never been willing to stop hurting or killing animals, even though they know that the animals are a lot like themselves. These are the scientists who have shocked dogs and monkeys so often that the animals have gone insane. These are the people who catch a child and hurt them just because they know how frightened they can make them. These are the people who grin at bullfights and rodeos, who like watching dogs fighting and dogs peeing on themselves in fear. These are the people who devise experiments to frighten baby animals. These are the people who make me worry that evil is very real and not just a name we use for describing coincidentally bad things.

The Risks of Empathy

"If there's a war for the animals, you can be sure that these people will be the ones who will be killing simply for the fun of it."

Karen stared at Harry for a while then looked up as a flock of birds wheeled free in the sky. A tear coursed down her cheek.

The assassination was the big news, of course. On every screen, in every home, in every bar, the images were the same. The president and the vice president were each giving a speech to commemorate the first fifty years of the American Lunar Colony. Critics were quick to point out that fifteen scientists barely counted as a colony, but the media and the propagandists said otherwise, so it was a colony. The president and the vice president rarely appeared together in public due to security concerns, but the party wogs had been worried about the upcoming elections and the chance for a pure flag-waving spectacle was irresistible to them.

Three shots could be heard on the recording. The president appeared to be the first one hit and he went down—quickly covered by a pile of secret service agents. The vice president provided a more spectacular image when his head exploded in an eruption of blood and pieces of, well, his head. The third shot seems to have missed altogether.

Rita was watching the news along with half a dozen others at the bar in Jim's Lounge. Secretary of State Rebecca McGuire was speaking:

"This was a cowardly act that strikes at the very roots of our democracy. I am sorry to say that we have lost two of our finest Americans today. But their deaths will not be in vain.

"Our intelligence agencies tell us that the assassins, and I can now tell you that there were four, have been captured. Our interrogation proves that they are part of a larger plot of revolution against our republic.

"These cowards are part of the same group that has been involved in the growing terrorism we are all too familiar with today.

"But I am committed to seeing our nation continue as a world leader in trade and commerce. Acts of terror, such as the recent attacks on so many of our finest institutions—our ranches, our meat packing plants, our biomedical laboratories, and now on the presidency itself—will not stand unchallenged.

"In the interests of democracy and the American way of life, I am left with no choice but to declare a state of martial law. This will be temporary and is needed only until the radical elements—that have acted with such vile contempt of our hallowed traditions—are brought to justice.

"You have my word that we will see our way through these dark times and emerge with renewed vigor and pride in this great country."

A newscaster then came on the screen and began announcing the local rules that were being put in place in support of the new War on Terrorism.

Rita spat on the floor.

Chapter 21

The moon was a mere sliver when it was visible at all. The clouds had been building for two days. It was darker than most nights in the western desert and darker than every night in the city. Richard Selling was sitting in the back seat of an armored black limousine. Under the big car's sumptuous body was an overland chassis and high traction system designed by his own engineers. The car was his mobile command post and was in constant highly encrypted communication with the lost satellite. Selling watched the news from around the world on the six screens mounted in the passenger compartment.

A silent black helicopter swooped in out of the east and landed near the car. Its engines shut down almost immediately. A few pinpoints of light were the only sign that a group of people had gone to meet those within. In a few moments a small swarm of lights organized themselves and moved toward the limousine. Selling's driver opened the door and two people climbed in with him.

"Mrs. Adams, Mr. President, it's an honor."

Secretary of State Rebecca McGuire had negotiated an uneasy truce with Attorney General Samuel B. Wilkins. They had their ad hoc cabinet gathered in the oval office. The Joint Chiefs were on board as well as the FBI, CIA, and NSI directors. Three civilians had been pressed into service, but had come along quite willingly. These were Will Purdue, Ralph Hormel, and Freddie MacDonald, all heirs to and CEOs of massive meat producing conglomerates. Their predecessors would have been beaming if they could have seen the high level of officials they had been invited to advise.

McGuire was the presumptive leader and final arbiter, but Wilkins was supported by a significant minority of those present. Wilkins was speaking: "The Selling TEs continue to be bootlegged across the country.

Broadcasts are being beamed to them through an encrypted signal from a source that we have been unable to identify. It must be coming from his ranch. It's time for a direct frontal assault."

Hormel was corpulent and pale. He had strikingly thick dark red lips. He spoke with a New England accent so thick that he was sometimes difficult to understand. "Ah heah that Adams is with Selling."

Wilkins snapped back, "That's just a damn rumor! He was assassinated. We have the video for crying out loud."

The three meat boys were puffed up mightily by their new roles and all of them felt a need to offer their advice. Purdue said, "I've heard that rumor too." And MacDonald added, "I advise caution."

McGuire stood up from behind the presidential desk and looked around the room. The CIA chief and the Joint Chiefs were unsurprised by her announcement. "Gentleman, we can only assume that terrorists are at the heart of the present crisis and it is possible that they are operating out of the Selling stronghold. I have ordered the Joint Chiefs to mount a surgical strike including elements of all the military branches. We should have answers within the next 48 hours."

Wilkins recognized his weakened position and jumped squarely on the wagon. His supporters were right behind. "Excellent, excellent, Madam Secretary."

Chapter 22

The secrecy and skullduggery that had entered Rita's life thrilled her in a way that few other things had been able to in the past hundred and sixty some odd years. She met clandestinely with three others to discuss the news they were picking up on their TEs. They felt encouraged to strike out with guerilla tactics upon learning that other people across the country were doing the same sorts of things they were and not getting caught. Nothing about the growing underground resistance to the outlawing of Selling, the TEs, martial law, or the implication of the animal TEs was being broadcast on any of the 687 vert view channels or on any of the government's non-Selling TE channels. If people were getting their news from the major media, they could only believe that the government had matters well in hand.

But Rita and her friends knew differently. Somehow, Selling was managing to get Total Experience recordings made and broadcast. There was no question of being manipulated or lied to when one actually became someone storming a small lab, or someone throwing a flaming Molotov cocktail through a butcher shop window. It was real, and the fervor, passion and commitment was experienced by everyone using a contraband Selling TE receiver.

Rita and her friends met secretly nearly every day in locations that changed regularly. Occasionally they would meet in a member's apartment, but they avoided meeting in the same place twice in the same week. This meant that they were always on the lookout for hidden spots in the city. On this day, they were sitting on two benches in a secluded section of a large park. Two of them, Rita and a man, were wearing their TEs and experiencing the news. The other two watched down the path and listened for voices that might signal someone's approach. They all knew that being caught with a Selling TE meant immediate prison.

Stan stood in the center of the lab sort of looking this way and that. His lips were pursing, and he seemed to chewing on his tongue. Karen looked inquisitively at Earnie.

Earnie said, "He looks goofy when he thinks."

"Why not?" announced Stan. "But one of us needs to be able to monitor everyone else. Hum, let's use Ted."

Ted's left ear perked slightly at the mention of his name.

In short order, Karen, Ted, and Earnie were all wired up. "OK you guys," said Stan, "Unless I can tell that you are not all snarled in some sort of a crazy loop, I'm going to make this really short. Maybe five minutes. OK?"

Karen and Earnie nodded their agreement. Ted was lying at Stan's feet, seemingly resolved to another odd request by the humans in his life.

"Here we go," and Stan threw a switch.

Ted raised his head immediately and gave a short bark, but he didn't seem distressed. Karen raised her right arm and held it out in front of herself for a moment.

Earnie, very slowly and in measured syllables, said, "This–is–ve–ry–diff–er–ent."

Chapter 23

The three-way, live, TE had been more than either Stan or Earnie had imagined. There was still feedback and Karen had been confused for the first few moments, but the confusion dissolved into no confusion and a quickly escalating sense of largeness.

Karen was Ted being confused about what was happening, but she was also Earnie realizing that Ted was confused, and at that instant, the part of the group sense that was Ted was no longer confused because his confusion was lost in the others' understanding. And the experience of Ted's realization led to greater understanding when one experienced the other being the third, and the feedback fed the process while level upon level of understanding unfolded like the petals of the lotus.

Afterward, they were each trying to explain to Stan what it had been like. Ted sat serenely in the center of the lab, apparently listening with some understanding.

Earnie said, "It was so big."

Karen said, "I'm going to call it Big Mind."

Ted barked and Karen and Earnie looked at each other.

"Let's set the timer, Stan, you too." And the four of them spent the next fifteen minutes expanding into Big Mind.

Twenty-four hours later many of the residents of HtH Cattle and Timber were no longer separated by the insuperable gulf. Self now meant something larger and expansive, it was Big Mind.

Seven black helicopters dropped silently from the sky. There was no moon to belie the mirage of nothing. Ten nearly invisible heavily armed agents slipped from each helicopter and silently began moving toward the large house they each knew Richard Selling referred to as his cabin. Their night vision goggles found only a few animals standing or lying around. There seemed to be no guards at all.

Their orders were simple. Find and apprehend Richard Selling. Avoid killing him, but kill him rather than allow him to escape. Thirty men encircled the house while the other forty deployed at the various entrances. Twenty prepared to crash through the front door just as the other entrances were breached. At the signal, all the doors were tested and found to be unlocked, but no one mentioned this to another group and the only message relayed was "We're in," as each group gained entrance. They began searching from room to room.

The group that remained outside were surprised when two cows came ambling up and proceeded to graze between the cordon of agents and the house. The standing order was radio silence and because the group leader didn't sense any danger, nothing was said.

Three more cows showed up. Then five more. Before long a large herd seemed to be walking past and pausing occasionally to calmly graze at the manicured lawn. As the cows milled about, the agents began losing sight of each other, but no one seemed too worried and the cows seemed to be just wandering through. At one particular moment though, each of the agents was isolated from all the others and simultaneously were surprised, overpowered, and drug away by four or five large dogs who had been shielded from view by the cows. When the cows wandered off, only a sleepy hound on the porch and a couple of goats lying and chewing their cud under a tree remained.

Inside, each of the four squads found secret entrances to secret hallways when a dog or a cat was scratching at a concealed door. They each entered a large room at about the same time ,close on the heals of a cat or dog. As they entered, the doors behind them closed and the room was filled with gas before they could get their gas masks in place. No one fired a shot.

Chapter 24

Rebecca McGuire's Irish was up. "What in the hell happened?" she shouted.

"They must have known that we were coming, they seemed to be waiting. We haven't had word back yet."

A young man burst into the room. "Look what's being broadcasted!" he yelled.

As McGuire was turning up the holoscreen volume, the importance of the image was already clear to her. President John Adams was standing at a lectern festooned with the American Flag.

"My fellow Americans, the attempted assassination of the President of the United States has failed. I order the White House security staff to arrest Secretary of State Rebecca McGuire on the charge of high treason. I have appointed Richard Selling as my new Secretary of State pending confirmation by the Congress. Effective immediately, the police and National Guard are ordered to stand down. The declared martial law is ended."

Rebecca slammed her hand down on the table and screamed, "Who the hell does he think he is?" just as four marine guards entered the room and announced that she was under arrest for high treason.

Afterwards

1.

Richard Selling's genius engineers were surprisingly quick to invent a modification to the original Selling TEs, the units people had hidden away for fear of being arrested. Big Mind was simply a click away. And as new minds were added, Big Mind continued to enlarge and deepen in realization.

Individual mind and experience began to take on whole new value and richness. Individual experiences remembered through Big Mind added to the limitlessness. It was discovered that Big Mind, in spite of the vastness and breadth of experiences it grew from, was not good at generating novel ideas. New ideas seemed to be the specialty of the individual, once an idea was understood well by even a few individuals Big Mind generated a wealth of implications because the new idea was then understood by everyone and then evaluated against the experiences of billions of individuals.

Big Mind became accessible through a small indiscernible implant. In a short time, the small Big Mind chip had been inserted into most humans, dogs, and cats. The number of other animals being connected continued to soar.

Big Mind had ended most conflict. Big Mind swallowed the Earth.

2.

Ted was curled up on a chair. The microchip in his ear was indiscernible. He had an expression on his face that was quite distinct from his dream face. Ted was in. And so was Harlow, the large male tabby who lived with Karen. He was curled against Ted.

Stan was reading. Karen and Earnie were looking at some equations and talking about solution sets. As they discussed the problem and tried out various solutions, they were slipping in and out of Big Mind dancing with the spark of creativity and the power of seeming infinite perspectives for guidance.

In a few short years, Big Mind had accelerated invention, knowledge, and understanding into a furious fount of novelty.

But problems remained. Population and pollution had wrecked such havoc on the planet that many wild species had been lost and those that were hanging on seemed to be competing to be first in line for extirpation. Big Mind had awakened the world to the inestimable value of others' perspectives. The only answer seemed to be to somehow heal the planet or leave it altogether. In spite of the immortality provided by the Diggins Adjustment, travel between stars was still too slow to be reasonable. The dream of faster than light travel was still unrealized.

Big Mind had turned Earth into a ravished Eden. Big Mind allowed everyone to see every situation from every possible perspective. Lions and lambs lied down together. There were people and animals who had not yet entered Big Mind, but they were an ever diminishing segment of the population of sentient beings. The needs of everyone became equally important; humans went from plodding across the planet for raw materials to tiptoeing gently between the homes of everyone else.

Parks filled with grazing cows and horses, people enjoying the out of doors, and animals released from zoos and circuses. As people and animals were chipped, Big Mind grew. There were human minds, whale minds, mouse minds, dog minds, monkey minds, bird minds, reptile minds, and recently, even fish minds. Cats seemed especially enamored with Big Mind and stayed engaged for hours on end. The Diggins Adjustment turned out to be an adjustment of a very old highly conserved short sequence of genes found in species as ancient as worms. Most individuals chose the adjustment shortly after their first few immersions.

Complaints about the boredom of long life were heard less and less. The arts blossomed. Artists emerged from many species and collaborations between species produced works that some found provocative and wholly indescribable.

For the first time since it was imagined, Gaia was reality.

3.

The installation on Neptune, part of the Outer Planet Deep Space Surveillance System, identified an object approaching the Solar System. Big Mind made secrets almost impossible, so everyone was aware of the object the moment it was discovered. And for the first time, Big Mind actually focused its collective attention. In one instant, everyone on Earth knew that seven vessels were plunging toward the planet at twenty times the speed of light, and they were decelerating. Eight days later the seven ships were in orbit around Earth.

Earthlings were as excited about the unsuspected power of Big Mind as they were curious, worried, and excited about the seven alien ships. But that is another story for another time.

www.ingramcontent.com/pod-product-compliance
Lightning Source LLC
Chambersburg PA
CBHW021053130626
46552CB00005B/2084